Cool Beans

Grinding Reality: Book Two

AJ Tillock

Cool Beans: Grinding Reality, Book Two

Cover by Steven Novak

Digital ISBN: 978-0-9836772-5-3

Print ISBN: 978-1-951286-00-2

1. Female Amateur Sleuth - Fiction 2. Contemporary Fantasy 3. Action/Adventure - Fiction 4. Albanian Mafia - Fiction 5. Coffee - Fiction 6. Florida – Fiction 1. Title

Chapter One

They are a stubborn, twisted generation

I pull jugs of white mocha sauce off the bottom shelf and set them on the floor. A thrill runs through me when I see the shiny silver bag. I sit cross-legged on the floor of the store room and pull the bag from its hiding spot, wedged between the bottom shelf and the wall. As always I ignore the "Do Not Open Do Not Use" stamp. I unroll the top of the bag and peer inside. The mysterious coating on each of the peaberry coffee beans glistens and sparkles.

I withdraw one and the ritual begins. I observe the bean closely as I hold it in the palm of my hand. What is it about these beans? Where does their power come from? For that matter, where had the beans themselves come from? They were unlike any others I'd ever seen. Of course, if I'd heeded the warning label, I wouldn't have seen them.

As the assistant manager of this Java Jake's, I have a perfectly legitimate excuse to be in the back room prior to opening. Dawn, who's out front, will never suspect a thing. No one else has even though I've had a couple of close calls since

I discovered the forbidden beans several weeks ago.

I swallowed the first bean accidentally, but after that I couldn't stop, even after I figured out what happens afterward. Now I know that within twenty-four hours, I will temporarily turn into...something else. When the effects of this bean wear off I will go back to being me. Until I swallow another one.

I've tried to resist, but the beans have a strange power over me. The longest I've gone without one is six days. By the seventh day I have to have one.

I slide the bean onto my tongue and close my eyes savoring every second. The coating never lasts long enough for me to define what it is or to compare it to anything I've tasted before.

This morning is no different. I swallow my disappointment along with the bean before I roll the top of the bag down. I shove it behind the shelf, replace the white mocha, turn off the light and open the store room door.

☐

Chapter Two

O foolish people,

The night time air is warm and humid and laden with moisture like it always is along the south Florida coast after one of the early evening summer downpours. I take in my surroundings as best I can in the semi-darkness. Perched amongst the fronds of a potted plant I have a spectacular view of a bottom-lit kidney-shaped swimming pool, the kind built for ambience, not for swimming laps. The area surrounded by a screen enclosure isn't very large but it is elegantly appointed with top-of-the-line resin furniture made to look like wicker appointed with rust-colored cushions. A couple of glass-topped tables and a small wet bar/grill ensemble complete the space.

I squirm around, to get a better look at my immediate situation. Wait. I know this place. I swivel my head which doesn't seem to have a very large range of motion. My gaze sweeps the patio area and beyond to the sliding glass door. Yes. I am sure of it. This is my sister Sammi's villa tucked inside a secluded gated community in south Seagate. She bought it a year ago when she finally felt secure enough with her real estate sales income to commit to a place of her own.

No one worked harder for financial security than Sammi. She sells high-end homes in Colfax County and she's good at it.

Question was what am I doing here? A better question is what am I?

Experimentally I lift a hand—er—foot and peer at it. Hard to be sure in this light, but where my hand normally is, I see a sort of greenish extension of my front leg with four suction cup toes. I take a step and the frond on which I'm balanced sways precariously beneath me. I get sickeningly dizzy for a moment, and hold on with everything I have. Funny thing was, hanging on was the easy part. No doubt due to my suction cup toes.

I hear voices from inside and glance up. I can see through the sliding glass into Sammi's home. There are lights on in there. I hear her voice and one other—a man. Sounds like he is trying to talk her into something. His voice is smooth and seductive, with a slight Latino accent.

I edge closer to the end of the frond causing it to dip and sway. It's wet, but I hold on, trying to get a better look inside. No such luck. I can hear the voices, but I can't see much. The slider offering the best view inside shows the kitchen and they weren't in there. Only a dim light over the stove is on.

Curious now, I slide closer to the edge of the frond. I'm not very far above the interlocking brick floor of the pool deck. Maybe three feet or so. There are more fronds below me. I can probably stairstep my way from one to the next all the way down. How hard can it be?

I gather my courage, focus on my target which is another frond maybe four or five inches lower and to the right. I brace myself, close my eyes, take a step and oops, uh-oh, yikes! I'm flying. Into space. I open my eyes as I slide off the leaf I was aiming for and a bunch of water droplets cascade down with me, down, through all of the other fronds below. I grab at them, but my suction feet are useless when I'm being propelled by the force of gravity and have nothing solid to suction to.

I land with an undignified *oomph!* on my rear end in the pile of wet mulch covering the dirt in the pot. If I could reach it, I would rub my sore bum. As it is, I'll know better in the future not to leap before I look. Or at least before I know what I'm doing.

See, here is my beef with finding myself in a new *entity*. My new temporary housing never comes with instructions. I'm usually flying blind, if I can fly at all, and also flying solo.

But I digress. My immediate problem is how to maneuver as a tree frog on wet, unfamiliar surfaces without severely injuring myself. One of the negative consequences of turning into other entities is that I sometimes retain the aftermath of what occurs when I'm in the body of something else. Like when I was a biting fly and I stung this guy Tyler's, um, well, I stung this guy Tyler, who thoroughly deserved to be stung because he was up to no good. He also deserved to be stung on the part of his anatomy where I stung him. But the next day? I could not get that metallic taste of blood out of my mouth. It was disgusting.

The night I turned into the cockroach and got burned because I jumped on Mr. Espresso Mafia's cigarette before he started the whole place on fire? I woke up with this oozing burn mark on my stomach. And I reeked! Who knew cockroaches smelled so bad? Thank God I didn't have to burn my favorite sheets.

Okay. Enough of the trip down memory lane. I crawl up to the edge of the planter and peer over the side to the pavers. Surely I can get down there without killing myself. Up and over the side. I could jump, I suppose. Or leap. Probably would be faster. But I wimp out. What can I say? I'm not feeling so confident about my leaping skills at the moment.

My suction feet work pretty well on the redwood planter even though it's wet. I make it to the bricks and pause for a moment trying to remember how far I'd ever seen a tree frog leap at one time. A couple feet, probably. The pool look enticing. I wonder if I'll be able to see my reflection in the water, dark as it is and with the water lit from underneath. Worth a shot. For some reason I always like to confirm what I think I am during these episodes. I don't know why. Not like I'm going to write a book about it or anything.

I poise myself and take a leap. I don't go very far, but at least I land pretty lightly on all fours. Good. I can get the hang of this. Another couple of leaps and I'll be at the edge of the pool. One. There we go. Leaping does not seem to come naturally to me. Okay one more try.

Oops. Shit. Overshot it. Stop. Stop. Stop! No brakes when you're flying through the air. I try to windmill to slow myself down. Uh oh. The edge of the pool flies by underneath me and then splash. Oh, no. Oh, rats. This is not good. I take in a big mouthful of water. Chlorine burns my eyes and my skin. Er—scales. Not good. Not

good. Get out. Get out. Now! I swim. Oh, God.
I'm a frog. I sure as hell hope I can swim to the
side before the chlorine eats me alive.

Panicked, I make it to the side of the pool.
Harder to get purchase now. My suction cups are
puckered and withering. I feel like I'm fading
from the dip in the chlorine. What will happen to
me if I can't get out of the pool? Eventually, the
effects of the bean will wear off. I'll turn back into
myself. Will Sammi find me floating in her pool
in the morning? No. No. Surely not. I'd go back
into my human body. Wherever that was. I'd be
whole again.

The decorative tile around the edge of
Sammi's pool is slick. I hang on for all I'm worth,
reaching, climbing, grasping, flexing my suction
cup toes, insisting they do their job. I try to slow
my breathing but I'm scared, damn it. Scared I'll
fall back into the water. Afraid I won't be able to
climb over the lip of the pool deck surrounding
the pool. Imagining Sammi's pool service coming
tomorrow with a skimmer and removing my
lifeless body. Tossing me in the trash. I'd be a
dead frog. Who would care? I had to get out of
here.

God, was this how Spiderman felt when he
was scaling those tall buildings? What about
those guys—where had I seen this?—with big

suction magnets or whatever, that held on to vertical surfaces? They had handholds so a guy could hang onto them and scale a skyscraper or something? The Discovery Channel, maybe? No. That Tom Cruise movie. *Mission Impossible*?

Focus, Tee. Focus. I grab and climb and suction for all I'm worth and finally make it onto the overhanging lip and back onto the flat surface of the pool deck. As I sit there trying to catch my breath, I'm not at all tempted to lean over the side to see if I can see my reflection. Okay. I'm tempted. But I'm not going to. I probably have a better shot trying to look at myself in the sliding glass doors anyway.

After a few minutes I recover from my dip in the pool and hop-walk over to the glass sliders. The hop-walk feels much more natural. The sliding doors set up a bit from the pavers so I crawl up until I can see inside. I'm too close to see my own reflection. I don't know why it's so important to me anyway. As a human who's lived her entire life in south Florida, I've seen tree frogs many times. So I can assume I'm a rather pale shade of washed-out green, that I have sort of slitted yet bulbous eyes and smooth skin—er scales. I've already discovered my suction-toed feet. No further confirmation of my appearance is necessary.

I cup my front set of suction toes around my eyes and peer into Sammi's dining/living area. Sure enough she is in there with a guy and he's putting the moves on her while she tries to squirm away from him. Shit. Please don't force me to be a witness to another near date rape. *Been there. Done that.* And especially not one involving my own sister.

Sammi is a grown woman, I remind myself. She's been living on her own since college. Although we don't discuss her personal life in detail, she seemed to go through men much the way our mother had: Quickly.

Sammi is an attractive, successful woman. More than attractive. She's gorgeous. Blond and built. Smart and sexy. Everything I'm not, as a matter of fact. Of course she has guys swarming her. Since junior high it seemed, she flirted, used and discarded men when she grew bored or another one snagged her interest. As far as I know, she never got attached to any of them. I don't remember her ever crying over one. In fact, I don't think she's ever been dumped. She moves too fast. She dumps men before they know what hit them. She's probably left dozens of broken hearts in her wake over the years.

But, back to business. I perk my hearing devices since I'm pretty sure I don't have conventional ears. How do frogs hear anyway? I'll have to look that up sometime. The guy is all over Sammi while she does her best to fend him off.

"Marco, just wait a couple of minutes. Let me check my e-mail."

"Check it later."

"I told you I've been waiting to hear from the seller's broker. I need this deal."

Sammi backed toward the desk where her laptop sat, even though he wouldn't let go of her entirely.

"Come on, baby. Don't be like that."

"Marco, stop it." Sammi actually sounds genuinely annoyed. I have to hand it to my sister. She's got good taste in men. This one is built like a romance novel cover model. He has longish, curly dark hair. Bronze skin enhanced by the sun. His shirt is unbuttoned. If I could, I'd probably drool just from looking at his bare chest. He's ripped and tanned and clearly he works out regularly.

Take it off. Take it off. Take it all off. That's what I'm chanting in my head. I don't have tons of experience with guys. I'm not a prude or anything, I just never quite got what the big deal was. No one's really tripped my trigger, yet, if you get my drift. Even as I think that, I think of Joe. Now he does it for me. I get giddy just thinking about him. He's not ripped like this guy. He doesn't exactly ooze sexuality, but he is sexy. I haven't seen Joe without a shirt, yet. I like to think we're playing it slow, but the truth is I don't know exactly what we're doing.

Sammi makes it to the desk, but Marco is right behind her. He isn't backing off at all. His hands are all over her and if I'm not mistaken, there's a bulge in his trousers. I edge a little to my right, and then a little more to try to keep an eye on them. I discover the slider isn't closed all the way. There is maybe an inch gap where it hasn't connected with the perpendicular metal track. In fact, there might be enough room for me to squeeze in.

I crawl over the cold metal, reach through to the inside, grasp the inside edge of the door jamb and scrunched myself through the narrow opening. The side of the door scrapes my back and the metal frame scrapes my tummy, but I make it in. I huddle for a moment. I don't know why my heart is beating so fast. Not like Sammi or Marco will notice me sitting here on the edge of the tile.

They are completely focused on other things. Sammi on her e-mail and Marco on Sammi.

"Hurry up," he whispers insistently as Sammi brings up her e-mail program.

She slaps at his wandering hands. "Knock it off." She concentrates on the list of e-mails in her inbox. Even I can't tell if she's truly annoyed with Marco or if she's playing hard to get. Is this a case of her lips saying no while everything else about her seems to say yes?

Marco doesn't back off. If anything, he gets more insistent. He drops his shirt and I get a nice look at his bare back. More muscle. Lots of smooth, tanned skin over it. He starts tugging at Sammi's top, trying to get it over her head.

"Marco," she warns. Annoyed? Or teasing? Still hard to tell.

Sammi opens the e-mail nearest the top and begins to read. She shrugs out of the blouse without comment. Marco lets it drop to the floor. Underneath the blouse she's wearing a white camisole. He starts fondling her again. She shrugs one shoulder like she's trying to shake him off. Then she stops reading and hits the reply key. Fingers poised over the keyboard she says to Marco, "I think it'd be best if you left."

"What?" Now *he* I could tell was definitely annoyed. His hands still.

"I've got a lot of work to do. I'm really not in the mood."

Hmm. Watching the two of them had done something for me. I think *I'm* in the mood. If

Sammi doesn't want Marco I wonder if she'd mind if I took a turn with him? Although me being a frog at the moment will be problematic.

"Let me get you in the mood, then, baby." He goes back to what he must have considered his surefire seductive technique. I wonder how long he and my sister had been seeing each other. Not long, I decide. Because if he knew Sammi at all he'd know an attempt to force her to do something she doesn't want to do will backfire. Usually in a most unpleasant way.

"Marco, it's not going to happen, tonight." This time Sammi put some force into her voice. She drops her hands from the keyboard and stands. "Put your shirt on and go."

"You don't mean that." I have to give him credit. He doesn't take no for an answer.

"Yes I do." Sammi sidesteps him, but he doesn't let go. "Marco, stop it." Now she's pissed.

Marco starts maneuvering her toward the bedroom with his body and superior strength. My blood starts to boil. What is it with these guys? Where is the fun in overpowering a woman, forcing yourself on her? I don't get it. Especially a guy like Marco who could probably have his pick of women. Tyler, too, for that matter. Either of them could probably find a woman who'd sleep with them willingly. So why pursue one who won't? It makes no sense.

Sammi does her best to dodge Marco's mouth and tongue, craning her neck this way and that every time he kisses her. He has her arms locked around her torso and effectively traps her against him. He is, in essence, dragging her to the bedroom.

Now I'm confused. Even though her body language seems resistive, she is quiet. Does Sammi really want him to do this? Is this some kind of game they were playing that I don't understand? Is Sammi a tease?

They are at the bedroom door before I gather my wits enough and decide I should follow. I do a couple of hop-step-leaps and I'm not far behind them. Marco gets Sammi inside the bedroom and kicks the door shut just as I take another giant leap to catch up.

I meet the solid wood panel full force as it swings back at the same moment I leapt forward. I slide down and land on the carpet. I think I had the wind knocked out of me. I wonder if I'll be bruised tomorrow, because hitting that door full on like that *hurt*. I lay there for a minute stunned, but I can hear rustling and struggling noises on the other side of the door. Then I hear material tear and my heart starts beating like a rabbit's.

Vaguely I wonder if I ever actually turn into a rabbit if my heart will beat the way I think a scared rabbit's would. How did anyone actually know how fast a frightened rabbit's heart beat?

There is a crack under the door, of course, about as big as the one I'd squeezed through before. The carpet is harder to crawl on because it's dry. I'm feeling rather thirsty. Like I'm drying up. I wonder how long a tree frog such as myself, surely used to more moist surroundings, will last in the dry barren landscape inside a house. My guess? Not long.

On the other side of the door and from the vantage point of the floor, I can't see much, yet I can see everything. Sammi's French provincial bedroom furniture, the silky spread that covers her queen mattress, and she and Marco still locked in either a struggle for control or a romantic embrace.

There is grunting, huffing and some muffled-sounding squeals, but whether they were squeals of delight or disgust I just can't tell.

I take a couple of half-assed leaps that put me at the base of the bed. Marco's pants are now pooled around his ankles and while I sit there debating about what to do and also admiring his muscular calves, firm thighs, and tight glutes covered by a pair of snug bikini briefs, he tumbles onto the bed and kicks his pants off so they drop to the floor. The weight of them settles over me before I realize what is happening and now I'm trapped under a pile of black poly-wool blend. As if that isn't enough, Marco's belt buckle beans me on the head. I'm not sure. I might have passed out for a minute or two. I panic. It's dark and hot and dry under here. Between the carpet fibers below me and the pool of material on top of me I think I'm going to suffocate.

Beyond that I can hear the sounds of movement on the bed, struggling and grunting and was that slapping? Were they getting violent with each other? Geez. I scramble and crawl and become more entangled in the material no matter which way I move. Then I realize instead of moving out from under Marco's pants I am actually crawling through one of the pants legs. I could go back and start over, I suppose, but I know if I keep heading the way I'm going, eventually I'll end up at the cuffed opening. I proceed, tripping over the folds, trying to straighten it out as I go, gasping for breath, unable to get rid of that panicky, claustrophobic feeling of being trapped. What if I can't find my way out? What if Marco finishes...whatever it is he intended to do with my sister and went to put his pants back on and out I tumble? A poor shriveled up little tree frog. He'd find me disgusting. I imagine him grabbing several tissues so he wouldn't have to touch me and carrying me at arm's length into the bathroom where he unceremoniously dumps me into the toilet. He wouldn't think twice about flushing my poor lifeless body into the sewer.

That thought propels me on, my heart racing once again, but not like a rabbit's I decide. Like the scared tree frog I am. I push and fight and gag breathing in the scent of Marco that clings to the inside of his pants. Man scent. That's all I can think. Not like he put cologne on his legs or anything. A hint of some metrosexual soap product, I decide. One of those guy body washes. Maybe a little guy perspiration mixed in. Everybody's body smells, doesn't it? We all have our own unique scent. Our own body chemistry. Frankly, Marco's doesn't smell too bad.

Finally, oh, my gosh, how long have I been stifling inside these pants? An hour? Probably not. But I can see the light at the end of the tunnel so to speak. I poke my nose out and breathe the slightly fresher and cooler air of Sammi's bedroom.

The struggle on her bed continued and I don't know why I can't hear voices. I'm not sure what I'm hearing. Lots of heavy breathing and movement. Are they...doing it? Where had Sammi's objections gone? Is she willing? Or is she being silenced? Only one way to find out. I eye the silky bedspread. Sammi has one of those pillow top mattresses that make her bed even higher than a regular bed. Frankly, after the pool, the jumping, the leaping, the fight to get out of the pants, the emotional stress of being here, watching my sister and Marco interact, trying to figure out Sammi's deal, I'm exhausted. Emotionally and physically drained. Hungry. Tired. Dry. I need some moisture. I think of the cool leaves of the dieffenbachia outside. By the pool. The deliciously moist fronds I'd slid off. Oh, they sound like heaven now. I'd head right back out there. As soon as I make sure Sammi is alright.

I'm no voyeur, but something doesn't seem quite kosher about this situation with Marco. Sammi is in fact, my baby sister, even though she acts older and is miles more sophisticated than me. I have some sort of misguided protective instinct where she's concerned, though God knows I couldn't protect her from much of anything because I myself am rather the screw-up. But still, I'm here now, and I'm not leaving until I assure myself all is well. Besides, the one thing I've discovered thus far about my transference into these other beings is that there's usually a reason why it happens. Why I end up where I do the way I do. Unpleasant as it often is, the end result is often positive.

Okay, then. How best to scale the slick silkiness of that comforter? I check my suction feet. Still there. Hopefully they'll suction onto the material and allow me to crawl up. I take a leap and barely catch the bottom hem. I hang on for dear life as the material sways a bit and then I start scrambling up. I sure was better at crawling than I was at jumping. I don't know what's wrong with me. Frogs jump, right? So am I some sort of defective frog? Maybe all my human inadequacies go with me when I go into another being's body? Because let me tell you, I can be pretty inadequate in human form, too.

It's like rock climbing to make it to the top of the mattress. The tumbling bodies on top of the comforter sure didn't help my cause. The whole way up the fabric shifted beneath me and I had to stop and hang on before moving up another few inches. But I reached the summit. From the bottom corner of the bed I surveyed the scene. Both Sammi and Marco are wearing a lot fewer clothes than they were last time I saw them. Sans shirt and slacks, the only thing covering Marco's rock hard ass are bikini briefs. They aren't leaving much to the imagination if you get my drift.

Sammi is down to her underwear and I gotta say, to me, it still looks like she's fighting him. But is she fighting fighting or play fighting? They're wrestling as best as I can tell. Sammi's bra is askew, but still intact. Almost like this is some sort of sex ritual they go through. They slap at each other, grab and pinch and God knows what else. Maybe it's nothing more than rough sex? Consensual rough sex?

I hear a ripping sound and every sense I have goes on alert. Sammi's underpants come away in Marco's hand and he sits back for a minute, straddling her. I have the feeling he's smiling for having destroyed her panties, but who knows? I creep closer because I can't help myself. I need to see Sammi's face, look into her eyes. Is she okay with this?

The rumpled bedclothes obscured my view of her. Now I see Marco has decided to divest himself of his briefs, or at least lowered them enough to—

"No. Stop, Marco. I'm not ready." This comes from Sammi and she sounds deadly serious to me.

"Oh, I think you're ready, cara," he insists. He too sounds deadly serious.

He starts pushing against her and, oh, God, I don't want to see this. I don't know what to do.

"Marco, stop. You're hurting me."

"It will be fine, baby. You'll see."

"Marco!"

Okay, that's enough for me. I poise, jump and somehow manage to land myself awkwardly on Marco's back. If he senses my presence he gives no indication. I crawl up his back. Surely each touch of my suction cup toes must feel like a caress to him, right? What guy wouldn't love that?

I get to his neck and continue up through his hair. He has nice hair. Thick. Dark. It smelled good, too. I wonder what kind of shampoo he uses? Conditioner? It smells like coconut. I make it through his hair and stop just above his forehead.

From there I can look down at Sammi and see whatever it is Marco would be able to see if he wasn't so intent on his own um, needs. Sammi doesn't look happy. She's bucking beneath him and still trying to push him away. I have to grab onto his hair to keep from falling off and the rocking motion is making me nauseas. I don't know what I'm supposed to do now. I have no weapons. I can't bite or sting. I'm a freaking frog for chrissakes! A stupid, useless, green frog who can't jump worth shit. I'm less than useless.

Then Sammi starts to laugh. That distracts me from my self-flagellation. It distracts Marco, too. I look down and even from this vantage point I can see his face redden beneath his tanned olive complexion.

Sammi loses control and Marco doesn't like it. She laughs hysterically and finally, she points at his head. She tries to speak, but between her laughter all I can make out was "Frrfrrrstg." Or something like that. Marco puts a hand to his head. I shift a bit to avoid his probing fingers, but he finds me. Oh, shit. *That's* what she's laughing at. *Me!*

I literally leap before I look. I have no idea where I'm going. I only know if Marco catches me, I'll be dead meat. For real. He'll eat my little froggy legs for dinner tomorrow.

Because I'm such a lousy leaper I almost knock myself out when I land on the headboard. I forgot to use my suction toes and I start to slide down, down, down, before I get my bearings. Marco is off of Sammi and after me so I turn myself around and crawl to the bottom of the headboard and then across to the leg. I make myself as tiny as I can on the back of the leg and take a few seconds to catch my breath.

The mattress shifts and I see Marco's bare feet. He's after me. Why, oh, why can't I be one of those big horned toads? Aren't there poisonous frogs or toads in south Florida? Don't any of them have teeth or spikes or anything of use against an enemy force? The only advantage I have is that I'm small. And green. Okay. Being green isn't exactly an advantage when you're trying to hide out in a pale beige French provincial bedroom suite. If only I were a chameleon. Now there is a creature with built-in protective gear. Nature's stealth. If you can't see me, you can't find me.

A shadow crept over me. More heart racing. Shit. It was Marco's hand. He'd found me. I panicked. I admit it. I crawled down to the carpet. I'm sure he thought he could trap me there under his hand. But I was quick. And I hope I am still relatively cool and maybe even a bit slimy. I jump onto his foot. That had the effect I wanted. It freaked him out. He let out a rather unmanly squeal.

He kicks out to dislodge me. Even though, frankly, if he hadn't he probably could have caught me before I gave one of my pathetic hops. But when he kicked out he propels me onto the dresser. I crawl quickly this time through the mess of girl stuff Sammi keeps there. Hair clips and discarded jewelry. A hairbrush and perfume bottles. A couple of scarves and bobby pins. I pause just a nano-second to stare at a small framed picture. It is the same one I have on my night table. I crawl up the mirror. At last I get a look at myself. I'm not pretty. In the mirror's reflection I see Marco, his um, package still hanging out of his briefs, coming after me. I crawl around to the back of the mirror and down, down, down the back of the dresser. What the hell. I crawl all the way down and get myself underneath it. There isn't much room, but there's enough for me. I'll be shocked as hell if Marco decides to move the dresser to find me.

"Nine-one-one operator. What is the nature of your emergency?"

What? Had Sammi called 911? Because of a frog? You've got to be kidding me.

"I have a potential domestic violence situation." She must be on her cell phone with the speaker on so everyone in the room can hear it.

"Samba," Marco hissed.

"I can send a car. What's your address?" The operator asked.

"A car won't be necessary," Sammi said. "He's leaving."

Carefully I creep out from under the dresser and around the corner of it, so I can see what's going on. Sammi had grabbed a robe and gestured to Marco and Marco, you got to hand it to him, was no dummy. He gathers his clothes and pulls them back on, though his eyes shoot sparks at my sister.

"Are you sure, ma'am. I have a cruiser in the area."

"Just stay on the line with me, if you could until he's gone and I lock the door."

"Don't you worry, *cara*," Marco hissed. "I'm leaving and I won't be back. You are one loco chick."

I stay where I am while Sammi follows Marco to the door and locks it behind him. I hear her thank the emergency dispatcher then disconnect.

She comes back into the bedroom and enters the adjoining bathroom. She doesn't close the door. Why would she? As far as she knows she's alone.

I abandon my hiding place and make my way across the carpet so I can see what's going on. I hear a drawer slide open, but then it's awfully quiet.

I peek around the corner of the bathroom door. From this vantage point, I can see Sammi has lowered the toilet seat lid and is sitting on it, the silky robe pooling around her feet. She seems to be concentrating awfully hard on something, but I can't see what it is. I sure don't want to startle her. I weigh my options. To my left is the vanity and there's a slight overhang at the bottom of the cabinet for me to sneak along the tile under it to get closer to her. Problem is, if I stay on the floor, I won't be able to see any better even if I get closer. Instead I decide to crawl up the back of the open door. Sammi won't be able to see me unless she closes the door, but I'll be able to see her.

By now I've got the hang of the crawling thing. I still think I should be able to hop or leap better than I can, but either I was defective or tree frogs aren't given to such endeavors. It didn't take long to climb up the back of the door. I peek around the edge once I've passed the doorknob figuring that will be high enough for me to see what Sammi is up to.

I suck in a breath. Sammi is bleeding! Oh. My. God. *What* is she doing? She has a razor blade in her right hand and she's made several thin incisions across the top of her left thigh.

Oh, Sammi, no! I want to wail and scream and thrash out at her. Why is she hurting herself? I stare at her. I think I forget to breathe for a minute. My beautiful, perfect baby sister who has it all together is cutting herself. I look closer at her bare thighs and see tiny white scars across them.

Oh, God. This explains why she never wears short shorts, always opting for skirts or capris. If she wears a swimsuit, it's a one-piece and she always wears a skirt wrap cover-up. I try to remember the last time I saw her get in a swimming pool. She has a knockout figure yet she never wears bikinis any more. I stare hard at her parted robe and I think I now know why. There are small white scars across her tummy.

Oh, Sammi, Sammi, Sammi. I want to cry. I know cutting is a way some people deal with emotional pain. Sammi is in pain, evidently, but I didn't know. She never confided in me. I'm not exactly a prime example of pristine mental health, so maybe that's why.

She'd left her cell phone on the counter and it began to play a few bars of Christina Aguilera's "You Are Beautiful" accompanied by a buzzing vibration. Sammi sucks in a surprised breath and lifts the razor blade. She stares for a moment at the droplets of blood she brought forth with her efforts.

The she swipes the phone's screen and says hello in a tone that almost sounds normal.

She has a brief hushed conversation with the other party and then disconnects.

She continues to sit on the toilet staring at her marred skin. I want to cry but Sammi doesn't appear to be feeling any emotion whatsoever. That worries me more than the cutting. I shift around because frankly, I am tired. I don't know how long I can keep myself stuck on this door. I don't like any part of being a tree frog.

After a few minutes Sammi reaches for a tissue from a box sitting on the back of the toilet tank cover. She presses it to the line of marks she made across her thigh. Her blood has already clotted. She blots at it with the tissue and then stands and tosses the tissue into the wastebasket. From another drawer she takes a washcloth and wets it. Then she washes away the dried blood.

Just as she leaves the bathroom, the doorbell rings. Now what?

Wearily I crawl down the door to the floor and hop-skip-crawl behind Sammi as she goes to the door. She gets there way before me, of course, being that her stride is about twenty times the length of mine. I clamber onto the coffee table so I can have a decent view of whoever her visitor is.

Sammi opens the door. A few murmured words are exchanged and then a woman enters and closes the door behind her. She frames

Sammi's face with both her hands and looks into her eyes. The woman's face is etched with concern. Then she kisses Sammi. No, not a friendly kiss, like a little peck on the cheek one friend might give another. This is a full-on full mouth kiss which I think may involve some tongue. Gross!

When the kiss ends, the woman and Sammi entwine their arms around each other. Sammi's robe is not tied and the other woman doesn't seem to mind that at all. They come toward me and I hunker down between a stack of magazines and a crystal bowl filled with potpourri so they won't notice me. Not that either of them would recognize me in my present form anyway. But I recognize the other woman and now I'm doubly confused not to mention doubly grossed out.

That other woman? It's my psychiatrist. Dr. Rosalind Parker.

Chapter Three

He gave each of them a supervising angel!

Here's the thing about my *episodes*. I have no recall of or control over the transformation. I sort of come to and I'm something else. If it happens at night, it's not so bad. I wake up and I'm in my bed and I'm human again. At first I wasn't sure if anything had really happened or I'd dreamt it. But it wasn't long before I knew the transformations had indeed taken place.

It's one thing to wake up in your bed alone and whole again. It's quite another to be walking up the stairs with grocery bags in your hands or waiting on customers at Java Jake's and all of a sudden *zap!* You're back in your body but you didn't even know you were gone.

I can't say exactly when I stopped being freaked out by the experience. I mean, I know it isn't normal to turn into something else and then turn back into yourself. I know it's the beans that cause it. I know it but I can't stop. I'm addicted to them. Now I'm starting to wonder what's wrong with me because it doesn't bother me that I'm addicted.

Shouldn't it?

This time when I fade back into myself apparently I'm in bed asleep and I don't wake up until my alarm clock goes off. It's four a.m. I have to open again today. Java Jake's opens at five a.m. and you'd be amazed how busy we are early in the day.

In the bathroom I flip on the light and check myself for telltale signs of last night's experience. I'm not green anymore which is cause for celebration. I look like myself: the elfin face, the too-big brown eyes and the uncontrollable curls and waves of hair. No matter what I do with my hair it doesn't cooperate. I think there's a good side to being a frog. No hair to deal with.

It takes me all of five minutes to do my morning routine. I hardly wear any makeup. I brush my teeth. Since my hair is hopeless anyway, I do the best I can with it and throw on my work clothes, a black shirt and khaki shorts. The only thing I notice that's slightly out of whack is the ends of my fingers. They still have that sort of suction cup look to them. I'm pretty sure that will wear off before anyone else notices. I'm also ravenously thirsty. I fill a big go-cup with ice and water and suck on it all the way to work.

Dawn's there waiting for me to unlock the door when I arrive. I like opening with Dawn.

She's doesn't like to talk in the mornings, which leaves me plenty of time with my own thoughts while I go through the routine of counting the safe and the tills and stocking the self-serve cooler with sandwiches, salads and yogurt.

This is what I'm learning about turning into some insignificant creature and witnessing things I'd never otherwise have the chance to: Knowledge is a dangerous thing. A powerful thing.

I think about how little I know about other people. Even my own family. I didn't know my mother lied about who my father really is and why he left us. I certainly didn't know my sister was what? *Bi*? Or that she cut herself.

One good thing about my bean addiction is it led to seeing my father again after all these years. He showed up twice, mostly to warn me away from the group of rude, apparently unemployed but always loaded with wads of cash foreigners we at Java Jakes dubbed the Espresso Mafia. They were a joke to us before I discovered they had ties to the Albanian Mob and were involved in some seriously evil and illegal stuff. I don't know exactly what my father's deal is or who he works for, but pursuing these Albanian Mob guys is what keeps me connected to him. I can't give that up. I *won't* give that up.

I haven't forgiven my mother for lying to me and Sammi all these years. For letting us believe my father abandoned us. He did leave but apparently he was still around in some ways. We just didn't know it. He certainly jumped in quickly when he discovered my interest in the Albanians. My mother told me about how my father ran into trouble all those years ago while searching for his sister who had disappeared. Is he still looking for her? Were the Albanians or their organization involved in her disappearance?

Whatever happened, it doesn't excuse my father for abandoning us, but it makes his reasons for doing so a little bit noble. The way my mother tells it, he had to leave in order to protect us. But what neither of them ever understood is how much Sammi and I needed our father.

I can't believe I bought Sammi's perfect façade for so long. But isn't that the way it is? People show you what they want you to see. Most of us don't bother to scratch below that surface until we have a reason. Sammi is hurting herself. She has some weird sexual practices. And she is apparently involved in some sort of liaison with *my* psychiatrist.

I can't say exactly why it bothers me so much except that as far as I know, the first time Dr. Parker met Sammi was when I was in counseling a few years ago. We had a few family sessions, Sammi, me and my mother, Dorothea. I always thought I was the one who was messed up.

Now I'm addicted to those damn forbidden coffee beans.

As to Sammi...I don't know how to play that at all. I'm not supposed to know that she is cutting herself or that she's bisexual. Is she? Or is she a lesbian? Then what was going on with Marco last night? I'd prefer everyone just pick a camp and stick to it. I have no problem with homosexuality. I like the lines to be clearly drawn that's all. Me? I'm heterosexual through and through. I know this without a doubt. Just one thought of Joe Warner and I melt. In case anyone needs proof.

I want to move forward with my investigation into the Espresso Mafia, find out what they are up to. They're a bunch of sleezebags, but dangerous sleezebags to be sure.

Speak of the devils. I walk out of the back room after I finish the deposit and there they are. Three of the Albanians. Dawn is working the espresso bar and one of our newer crew members, Carly, is at the register. I move behind her to have Dawn witness the deposit in the cash management log. I do my best to ignore the Mafia guys, but Carly is having trouble understanding their orders.

"It's an espresso macchiato?" she asks, ready to mark the cup. "No foam, did you say?"

"Coffee and milk," says the one with the shaved head.

"He wants whole milk," I inform Carly. "He doesn't like to tell you that until after you make it wrong, though. Isn't that, right?" I direct that last line to him. We engage in a brief staredown. I'm not sure which of us won. I am sick of these guys with their attitudes and their wads of cash, their chain-smoking, non-English-speaking, messy gatherings on the outside patio. One way or another, I will rid Seagate of their presence entirely. I'll find out what they're up to and I'll put a stop to it. Even if I have to do it all by myself.

His scrawny companion sets a bottle of Perrier on the counter. "American coffee," he says to Carly.

Duh, I mutter under my breath as I turn to the coffee urns behind her. Why do they call it *American* coffee? Where do they think they are? Canada?

"Anything else?" Carly asks sweetly as I set the coffee on the counter. The third guy had apparently ordered first and has already wandered away to the hand-off plane.

Baldy stares at me as he peels a twenty away from a fat roll of cash and tosses it onto the counter. I stare back. Carly, unperturbed by his rudeness, plucks the bill up and makes change. "Thank you very much. Have a nice day," she says.

He ignores her, but addresses me. "You have nice day." He smiles at me revealing tobacco-stained teeth. Something in his eyes and his tone gives me the creeps. I drop the deposit into the drawer of the safe and go to relieve Dawn for her meal break.

When she comes back I give Carly a ten-minute break and then I go to lunch. Even though it's only ten-thirty, a sub from the deli at the Presto supermarket next door sounds good to me.

When I reach the plaza's covered walkway I realize the Espresso Mafia guys are still there. Java Jake's has small tables lining each side of the walkway as a designated smoking area. Because there are no other store entrances between us and the Presto, it makes sense. There is another seating area closer to the entrance of our store as well designated for non-smokers.

The members of the Espresso Mafia chain-smoke, so of course, they always take tables along the walkway. Sometimes there are six or eight of them and they rearrange the chairs and the tables to their own satisfaction and leave it that way when they depart. They also leave their overflowing ashtrays and empty cups and crumpled cigarette packages.

While I prefer not to have to walk past them to get to the Presto, other than take a circuitous route through the parking lot and make my discomfort with them obvious, I have no choice. I adjust the strap of my bag over my shoulder and start walking.

They break off their rapid-fire conversation in Albanian and all three of them watch my approach. The scrawny one has to turn around in his chair. I keep my head up and pretend they aren't there and that I haven't noticed them until I'm a couple of feet away. I make eye contact with Baldy. I hope what he gets from me was *I'm not afraid of you guys*. What I get from him is the same creepy feeling I always get. His assessing stare is a mixture of condescension and lewdness. Like he wonders if I'd be worth his trouble.

I walk on by and don't look back even when I hear a chair scrape against the tile. Presto's double doors whoosh open for me and I head to the deli. There is no line at the sandwich counter but I have to wait for one of the deli people to notice me and meander over to make my sandwich. I glance around while I wait. That's when I notice Scrawny a few feet away near the cold case displaying chicken wings and salads and pre-made sandwiches. He doesn't pretend to be looking at the food. He stares at me so I stare back. I know if I let these guys intimidate me one little bit, there will be no end to the harassment they'll dish out.

"What can I get for you?" The hair-netted deli guy whose name tag says "Chris" asks me a minute later.

"A six-inch roast beef on whole grain. Deli mustard, provolone, lettuce, tomato and pickles."

While Chris goes to work on my sub I glanced back at Scrawny. He is still watching me, but when I catch his eye this time he looks away, first over my shoulder, then at the food in the case nearest him. I turn my attention back to the preparation of my sub, but I can't help the little smile curving my lips. If I had to guess, I'd say none of these guys know what to do when a female refuses to be intimidated by them.

Whatever they dish out, I can take. They can try to make my life miserable. I'll find a way to turn the tables on them. If I'm uncomfortable, so will they be. Until eventually I bring this ragtag Southwest Florida arm of the Albanian Mob to its knees. I refuse to consider any other option.

When I get in the express line to pay I see Scrawny duck out the door. He is back at the table with the other two and again they all watch as I traverse the walkway back to Java Jake's. I wouldn't put it past them to do something juvenile like stick a foot out to trip me, so I stay as far from their table as I can get. But I do the stare-down thing again with Scrawny because he is facing me.

As soon as I'm past their table, one of them, Baldy probably, says something loudly in Albanian. The other two guffaw. I know it was about me but it's anyone's guess as to the context. I take a seat in the outdoor non-smoking section and unwrap my sandwich. I will not let these guys get to me. I might not have ruthlessness on my side but I am smarter than they are. I also have the power of the forbidden beans. A formidable opponent, that's what I am, whether they realize it or not. That's how I see myself. That's how I'll beat them.

When I wake up the next morning I start a pot of coffee and pull out a pen and a notepad to make a list. First I need to investigate self-defense classes and enroll in one. I am not going to be caught unaware the next time one of those Espresso Mafia goons come after me. I need to get a gun, learn how to use it and get a license to carry concealed for the same reason. These guys mean business and if I'm going to find out what they're up to and bring them down, I'll have to be as tough and mean as they are.

I put a croissant in the toaster oven and pour my first cup of coffee, doctoring it with a little cream. I savored the aroma for a minute and sip it while I continue with my list.

Make an appointment with Dr. Parker a few days from now after I cool off.

I need a computer as well. How I am going to afford one after I pay for self-defense classes and a gun and a permit for the gun, I don't know. None of those things are exactly in my budget.

Magic chooses that moment to make an appearance. He sends a minor hiss in my direction and then walks regally to his food bowl while holding his tail up stiffly. "Good morning, Magic," I greet him sweetly. "Did you sleep well?"

He sends me a sideways glance before settling down to his food bowl which I keep filled with dry food.

I go back to my list. I don't like anything I've written on it. Truth is I don't want to know anything I know as a result of turning into something else and being given the knowledge I otherwise wouldn't have. If I didn't know about those Mafia guys, I wouldn't feel compelled to find out what they were doing and put a stop to it. I could just go on hating them for being rude customers at Java Jake's. I wouldn't need a gun to protect myself.

The things I now know about my sister? I really, really don't want to know. Instead of feeling powerful with my knowledge, I feel helpless.

I have to stop the bean addiction. I write that down at the bottom of my list in capital letters and then I trace them over and over and over and over again: NO MORE BEANS.

No matter how hard it is, no matter if I hear them calling to me, no matter how drawn to them I am, I will not consume another one. I know too much about too many things I don't want to know about. I wasn't a huge fan of myself before the beans, but I desperately want to go back to the place I was before I'd ever opened that forbidden bag.

While I'd been able to infiltrate the Espresso Mafia while under the influence of the beans, that didn't mean I couldn't continue to pursue those guys, spy on them, learn more about them without the beans' help.

I nibble on my croissant and think about how best to deal with my addiction. Just say no. Ha ha. I wonder if they still teach that to kids in the DARE campaign like they did when I was in middle school. For all the good it did. I'm pretty sure there isn't a twelve-step program for magic coffee bean addicts.

Which makes me wonder. Am I the only person who's discovered a bag of those beans? What if there are others like me? Fellow Java Jakians in other stores in other places who've come across a forbidden bag of beans, who've opened them and let their curiosity get the better of them. Who are now addicts just like me.

An interesting thought but how can I ever find out? Not like I can go around with a survey. I couldn't even convince my shrink that the beans had this magical effect, that they temporarily turned me into something else. If I start babbling about my experiences, I'll be considered certifiable for sure.

I'm not crazy. I wrote that down on my list, just to reinforce it in my own mind.

I have a closing shift tonight, so I don't have to be at work until two this afternoon. That means I have time to go to the library and use one of their computers to do some research. I clean up my breakfast mess and jump in the shower. I decide to check on Cody before I leave, see how he's doing and if he needs anything while I'm out.

I knock on his apartment door across the hall from mine and he answers it pretty quickly. His face is healing nicely. The swelling is down. He has the stitches covered with a bandage, but otherwise he looks almost normal again. He's wearing nicer clothes than he usually does. A tie dangles around his neck. I don't think I've ever seen him wear anything other than his uniform or tee shirts and shorts or jeans. This more formal look is new.

"Job interview?" I quip.

He steps back to let me in. "Close. Meeting with a lawyer first and then Internal Affairs. Depending how it goes, I might be job-hunting later."

"Are you serious? Randall Grimes did that to you, and you can get fired for it?"

Cody steps into the bathroom to tie his tie in front of the mirror. I lean against the doorjamb and watch. "They're talking to everyone who was on the Randall Grimes detail that night. Did we follow procedure? What was the sequence of events? Why didn't anyone go back and check on him before it was too late."

Cody struggles to tie the knot in the tie. He yanks it out and starts over.

"Have they determined the cause of death yet?"

"Cardiac arrest. They're more interested in what exactly caused it. Results from all the tests aren't in yet."

"Surely they don't think you're responsible. He took you out the moment they took the shackles off him."

Cody stops fussing with his tie and turns to stare at me. "How do you know that?"

Because I was there. Hiding under the sink in my Black Widow spider disguise. "Um, oh, well, I don't. I just assumed." Yikes! I need to watch my mouth.

To distract Cody I step into the bathroom. "Here, let me do this." I take hold of the dangling ends of the tie and begin the process of creating a perfect Windsor knot.

Cody stares at me. I don't know how I know he is frowning since I keep my eyes on what I'm doing, but I can tell. I ease the knot into place and step back. "There. Perfect."

Cody turns to look at himself in the mirror. "Where'd you learn to do that?"

"That six-month stint working in menswear at Macy's." Just one of the jobs on my rather impressive list of short-lived career opportunities.

"Thanks." We exit the bathroom. Cody picks up a sports coat from where he'd draped it over the back of chair. "What are you up to today?"

"Off to the library to use a computer. I work at two."

He picks up his keys and wallet from the counter. "You can use mine if you want to. Unless you're planning to order sex toys or download porn."

"Ha ha. No. Just a few things I want to research. Like the best deal on a new computer."

He gestures to the desk in his bedroom. "Have at it. Lock up when you're done."

"Thanks. Good luck today."

I hear his key turn in the lock when he leaves and I bee-line to his desk. Cody's bedroom is pretty neat considering he's a guy. He doesn't exactly make his bed, but he straightens it up and yanks the navy-blue comforter over the sheets and pillows. He needs to dust and vacuum, but what single guy doesn't?

I boot up his laptop and get online. First I look at handguns. I want something lightweight. Easily concealed. It can't be too noticeable and weigh me down. No prices online. Not like you can buy a gun through the internet. So I look up gun shops in the Seagate area. There are several possibilities, from retail outlets to pawn shops. I make notes on my to-do list page about a few of them. Seagate isn't huge and I've lived here my whole life. As long as I have a street name or a general vicinity, I'll be able to find these places.

I look up what's involved in obtaining a license to carry a concealed weapon. I'm not even sure I need one, but it doesn't look too complicated if I decide I do.

Next on my list is self-defense classes. There are a few, mostly through the places that teach karate and jiujitsu. There are a couple taught by former cops, too. The county sheriff's office also offers classes in basic self-defense. Those are the cheapest option. *Your tax dollars at work.* I can start there and get into the more complicated stuff later on.

I need to start working out, tone up my muscles, build up my endurance. I don't know why I think this. In case I ever have to run for my life? Even if I give up the beans, I won't stop pursuing the Espresso Mafia. I'm still dying to know exactly what illegal stuff they're into. Especially if they're importing young women from Eastern Europe and forcing them into prostitution. Plus pursuing the Mafia means my father might make another appearance in my life.

While I have the computer available I look up cutting. I haven't fully committed to confronting Dr. Parker about her relationship with my sister. But I need to know more about Sammi's condition. What I read is disturbing as are some of the pictures of cutters. Some of them do real damage to themselves while seeking a release from emotional and psychological pain. As I suspected, someone like Sammi does not want attention. She'd be embarrassed and ashamed to reveal what she is doing. Maybe that's why she connected with Dr. P. For help.

After reading about cutters I decide the best the thing I can do for Sammi is try to be the kind of sister she needs. Supportive, understanding, caring. We are very different people and lately we haven't been particularly close, but that can change. I can try to change it.

I promise myself I'll call Sammi this week and ask her to go shopping with me. Like my mother, Sammi loves to shop. I'll pretend I need a new outfit for a date with Joe. Not that I can afford to buy a new outfit. So I'll have to pretend I don't like anything I try on. If only Sammi was the kind of sister who would go gun-shopping with me.

Chapter Four

For they are a stubborn, faithless generation

When I get off work that night some of the Espresso Mafia are still sitting outside in the smoking section. Four of them have been gathered around one of the tables for the last couple of hours.

I have no idea how long they normally sit there after we close because I never hang around long enough to find out. But tonight I decide I will. Katie and I leave the store together. She bids me goodnight and veers off toward her Mini Cooper. I get into my Jeep, a plan formulating in my head. On the corner at the front of the plaza is a gas station/food mart with a McDonald's tucked inside. I go through the drive-up window and get a Coke and some fries. Then I park several lanes away in front of the big new gym that opened in the plaza where a craft store went out of business a year ago. From here I can still sort of see what is going on in front of Java Jake's without being noticed. The gym is open until eleven and there are quite a few cars parked in the lane I'm in. I should probably join the gym if

I'm serious about getting in shape. They've been hawking cheap grand opening membership rates for months. Frankly, if I'm going to take up jogging, I'd rather do it on the beach than on a treadmill.

Another thing for my list. Binoculars. I should have looked those up while I was using Cody's computer. I have no idea how much they cost. Maybe I will check at a pawn shop when I go gun-shopping. Maybe I can get a deal.

I slink down in the seat and munch on the fries, which are lukewarm and don't have enough salt on them. They never do and I always forget to ask for extra. I yawn because I'm tired. And bored. Those guys could sit there until two in the morning. I don't relish the idea of sitting here until then. Plus, they will notice me if I do because there won't be any other cars in the parking lot. Except for theirs and my yellow Jeep.

I ball up the bag the fries came in and toss it on the passenger seat. I take a sip of my soda and perk up. They are breaking up. I squint to make them out as they split off in twos. The pair closest to me head toward an older black Mercedes. I lose track of the other two. I can only follow one car. Unless I call for back-up. The thought makes me smile. Like I have a whole crew behind me.

Lenny, maybe, would help me. But if I call him now by the time he arrives they'll be long gone.

I start the Jeep and back out. I don't want to get too close to them just in case they know who I am and what kind of vehicle I drive. I decide to stay back fairly far. If I lose them, I lose them.

They don't seem to be in any particular hurry to arrive anywhere, nor do they appear to be trying too hard to shake me assuming they know I am following them. They drive all the way out to Pointe Royale. I have a moment of panic when I realize that's where they are going.

Instead of following them when they turn onto Gulfshore Drive, I make a last-second turn into Valencia Plaza's parking lot. They'll have to come back this way and turn back up Crayton Road to get out of Pointe Royale. I find a parking spot with a good vantage point and sure enough about ten minutes later I see the Mercedes. I give them some lead time before I fall in behind them.

I try to keep at least one car in between my Jeep and the Mercedes. Before I realize it, we are in an outlying, mostly undeveloped area along the northeast border of Colfax County. There are very few houses and no streetlights except at the occasional intersection of county roads. There is also very little traffic. It is after midnight. I have to pee. The gas light on my dashboard has been on for at least thirty miles.

I'm pretty sure those guys in the Mercedes are leading me on a goose chase. I should call it quits, turn around, stop for gas somewhere, go home and go to bed. There will be other opportunities to follow them. I don't have to do it tonight.

Up ahead I see their taillights glow bright red as they brake and make yet another turn. Screw it. I'm done. I slow and U-turn right there in the middle of the road. I don't get very far before the Jeep's engine begins to sputter. I pull over to the soft shoulder just as it completely dies. I stare at the little gas tank light and the line where red glowing squares show how much gas is left. There are no glowing squares.

I glance in the rearview mirror. If those guys want to ambush me, I've given them the perfect opportunity. All they have to do is turn around and come after me. But I don't see any lights heading toward me. I turn off my headlights and put on my emergency flashers. For all the good it will do me. This late at night on this deserted road? Who is going to happen along to help me? No one that's who.

I dig my cell phone out of my purse and scan through my contact list. Who can I call? Cody?

He'll come, but he'll come armed with a lecture and a warning. He'll want to know what I'm doing out here and if I don't tell him, which I won't, he'll get suspicious and then he'll get pissed off. Joe? Joe would be here in a heartbeat, I know he would. He'd also have questions. I've been pushing the Joe-I'm-not-crazy envelope since our first date and I'd really prefer not to push it again. My sister? No. Dorothea or Patrick? No. Any of my other friends will probably help me, but I'm not that close to most of them. It's one thing to hang out and drink beer and play pool with them at Pelican Harry's. It'd be weird and awkward to ask them for a favor at midnight. Lenny? I don't think twice. In fact I'm not that far from Lenny's place. I wouldn't be surprised if he's still up. He'd be thrilled to hear from me no matter what the reason. If he helps me, I'll owe him, and we both know it. I made good on my debt the last time he helped me out. I'll do it again.

I dial his number and get his voice mail. I leave him a message anyway, without going into detail, asking him to call as soon as possible, and that I need his help.

Now what? I check the bars on my phone. It still has juice and luckily is getting reception. I'm back to a choice between Joe and Cody. Cody already knows I'm a little crazy and so far, he puts up with me in spite of it. I cross my fingers that involving him this little escapade won't change that.

Almost an hour later, I rouse when headlights shine in my rearview mirror nearly blinding me as a car pulls up behind me. When its interior lights come on I breathe a sigh of relief and open my door.

"What the hell took you so long? I thought you were never going to get here."

Cody doesn't answer. Instead he goes to his trunk and withdraws a gas can. In the light afforded us by his headlights I can tell by the set of his shoulders and the way he holds himself he is *pissed.*

"Sorry. Thank you for coming. I just didn't think it'd take you that long."

"Pop your gas cap."

I open the door and release the lever. He removes the cap and starts emptying the gas from the can into my tank.

"Cody, I—"

"Don't. Just don't."

"Don't what?"

He glares at me. "Don't lie to me."

That takes the wind out of my sails. I'm not even sure what I was going to say before he interrupted me. I feel tears well. I don't cry. I never cry. But the thought of losing Cody's friendship, well, that about kills me. He's been nothing but good to me and for me. He is the big brother I never had. If he turns his back on me, I don't know what I'll do.

"Sorry." It comes out shaky. I sniff. I turn around and swipe at the stupid tears with the back of my hand.

I can hear him finish with the gas and replace the cap. "I got held up on County Barn Road because there was an accident. A bad one. A pickup truck went through that embankment near Everglades Boulevard and flipped over. They were putting the driver in the ambulance when I got there."

His voice is almost normal as he tells me this. I turn around sensing there is more. We stare at each other for about thirty seconds. "It was Lenny, Tee."

"Lenny? Oh, God, is he—is he..."

"He was still alive when they left the scene. That's all I know."

You mind your own business and stay out of ours. Go back to pouring coffee. Be a good girlie or you and that boyfriend of yours won't like what happens next. That's what the guy had said to me after he beat me up. I didn't recognize him but I knew he was one of them, part of the Espresso Mafia organization. At the time I'd wondered who he meant when he referred to my boyfriend. Joe? Cody? Or Lenny?

I have absolutely no proof the Mafia was behind Lenny's accident. All I have is a gut feeling that told me of course it was them. The Mafia couldn't possibly know that Lenny wasn't my boyfriend. Could they?

"I have to go to the hospital."

"I'll go with you," Cody called. "Stop and get gas first."

I wave at him as I get in the Jeep and haul ass back into town. I really need Cody on my side. So I stop at the first gas station I see and fill up.

Chapter Five

For my anger has kindled a fire

Adrenaline buzzes through my system by the time I reach the hospital emergency room waiting area. I'd grabbed a cup of probably the worst coffee I'd ever tasted at the gas station. I drank the whole thing, my mind racing, every nerve on high alert.

Why would the Mafia target Lenny? He hadn't done anything except some research online which he'd shared with me. But that was weeks ago. Yes, he came over and stayed with me that one night after the beating, but again, that wasn't such a recent event. Yet I have this nagging feeling that his accident was no accident and that they'd been behind it.

I look around the waiting room trying to calm myself and get my bearings. Cody enters and comes up behind me right about the time I spot Lenny's mother, Shelly Shutzel. I'd met her exactly once, at his father's birthday party a few weeks ago. Although she'd told me at the party to call her Shelly, I can't. "Mrs. Shutzel?"

She glances up at me, a tentative smile on her perfectly made up lips. She is dressed casually, but expensively in slacks and a pretty silk blouse that complements her eyes.

"You probably don't remember me, but—"

"Yes. You're Scott's friend. Tee, isn't it?"

"Yes ma'am." I turn to indicate Cody. "This is my friend Cody Cavallero. Cody, this is Lenny—er, Scott's mother, Shelly Shutzel." Lenny had been christened Scott Leonard Shutzel, but he used his middle name professionally.

Cody nods at her. "Pleased to meet you."

She nods back and offers him that same tentative smile.

I take a seat next to her. "How is Lenny?"

"I don't really know. Steve's in there with him. He'll be out as soon as he can."

As if she'd conjured him out of thin air, Lenny's father, Dr. Steve Shutzel bursts through the restricted area of the treatment center. Shelly stands and so do I. He takes his wife's hand. "He's going to be okay. He's pretty banged up and he's got a concussion. He was lucky. He was wearing his seatbelt and the airbags probably saved his life."

"Oh, thank God." Shelly edged closer to him and he put his arm around her. He looks at me. "Tee, isn't it? Good of you to come."

"I just—I needed to—can I see him?"

"Probably not tonight," Steve replies. "They're transferring him to a private room. He's still pretty out of it. Why don't you come back tomorrow? I'll let him know you were here." His gaze takes in Cody as well. "Both of you."

"I'm sorry. Dr. Schutzel, this is my friend Cody Cavallero. He's with the sheriff's department and he passed the scene of the accident right after emergency vehicles arrived."

Dr. Shutzel and Cody shook hands. Dr. Shutzel gave us both a curious gaze, but he didn't say anything else.

"I'll—we'll come back and visit Lenny tomorrow. Would you let him know that we were here and—" And what? "Tell him I was worried about him?"

"I'll be sure to let him know," Shelly assures me.

"Thank you." I look at Cody. There's nothing else we can do.

Outside there are a couple of sheriff's deputies.

"Wait here," Cody orders me.

"Yeah, right," I mutter and fall into step next to him. He stops and turns. Something in his expression makes me back down. Not that I'm going to be gracious about it. I huff out an exaggerated sigh of resignation. "Fine."

He crosses to the two deputies who look like they're ready to leave. An animated five-minute chat ensues between the three of them, none of which I can hear, before the deputies get in their patrol cars and leave.

If possible, Cody looks even more grim than he did before. We start back to where our cars are parked.

"So?" I finally ask when he doesn't say anything.

He stops next to my Jeep. "I don't know what you got Lenny involved in, but he could have been killed."

"What? Me? I didn't—"

"Save it, Tee. Somebody was playing a game of chicken with Lenny tonight. There was a witness, another driver, too far behind Lenny's truck to see what actually happened, but he swears there was another vehicle that swerved back into the other lane once Lenny veered off the road. He didn't realize what had happened until he saw Lenny's truck. You don't want to tell me what's going on, that's your business, but don't call me next time you need help."

"I don't know why you think this is my fault," I say sulkily.

"And I don't know why you think I'm some kind of idiot," Cody explodes. "You've been acting weird for weeks now. You've got this bug up your butt about those Albanians." *No pun intended*, I insert silently. "Lenny was acting all cagey about why that guy forced his way into your apartment and beat the shit out of you."

"That wasn't—"

"Don't ask to use my computer again, either. Guns, Tee? Carry concealed permit? Self-defense classes? I don't even want to know what 'no more beans' means." He takes my list, which I must have left next to his laptap, from his pocket and shoves it at me. "What the hell is going on with you? What were you doing that far out of town on a deserted road in the middle of the night? Were you meeting Lenny?"

While I make a mental note to erase my browsing history and not leave a paper trail behind should I borrow a computer again, I try to formulate answers that won't be outright lies but which will satisfy Cody. I must have taken too long, because he gives me another one of those looks I don't like and says, "Forget it, Tee. I'm done. I'm going home."

He gets into his car and leaves me there, which I'd never in a million years thought he'd do. He's a cop and the closest thing I have to a best friend. That he doesn't want to make sure I get home safely, not tonight anyway, hits me where it hurts. A lump works its way into my throat and I blink back the tears that try to make another appearance.

I am bone tired, frustrated, worried and a little bit scared. I know what I've done to earn the ire of the Espresso Mafia, but what did Lenny do to warrant such deadly attention?

I already agreed to have dinner with Joe the next night, and even though after working eight a.m. until four p.m., all I want to do is go home and sleep, there is no way I will cancel on him. I make it through my shift with dose after dose of caffeine. I resist the urge to open the storeroom door, lock it behind me and get out my lovely bag of forbidden coffee beans. I fantasize about doing it, gazing at the beans with their sparkly coating of what I now think of as fairy dust. I visualize myself withdrawing one, holding it in my hand, studying it as if that would help me unravel the mystery of its magical power. Then finally, oh, finally, I will allow it to touch my tongue. I'll try to define the flavor of that magical coating. The coating never lasted long enough for me to get a handle on it. I think that is part of the appeal of those beans. That I hadn't gobbled up more than one at a time sometimes surprised me. Except after I'd figured out that they were causing my transformations, I was afraid to consume more than one, even if it would help me figure out what the coating was. What if consuming more than one made the transformations last longer, or made me temporarily turn into something huge, like an elephant or a whale? I could scare the crap out of myself imagining what could happen. Already I'd escalated from the insect world to the amphibian world. I didn't want to move up to the next category, whatever that might be. Nope. I was going to quit those beans cold turkey before I turned into one. I planned to forget I'd ever tasted or swallowed a forbidden bean. I'd pretend they weren't even there. At least I'd try.

When I get home, I take a shower. It revives me a little. I drink a Coke, as if I haven't had enough caffeine and sugar in the past eight hours. I know I look exhausted. I can't quite cover the circles under my eyes, but I give it my best shot with my limited supply of makeup.

Joe rings the bell and I answer the door. He steps inside and embraces me and kisses me. Even in my exhausted state, I respond, because frankly, Joe does something for me no other guy ever has. After a little bit he lets go and we sort of stare at each other. "I missed you," he says.

"Me too." That is a lie. When I'm with Joe, I'm abuzz with attraction feelings. But when I don't see him or talk to him, sometimes for days at a time due to our conflicting schedules, I don't spend a whole lot of time thinking about him.

My stomach gurgles. I haven't eaten much, so focused have I been on keeping caffeine circulating through my system. I am starving.

Joe grins at me. "Someone's hungry." He takes my hand. "Come on. I'll feed you."

On the way to his car I say, "Do you mind if we make a stop first?"

He unlocks his car with the remote and opens my door for me. "Not at all. Where?"

"I need to go see Lenny."

He give me a pained look before he closes the door and walks around to the driver's side. Joe and Lenny like each other but they kind of consider themselves rivals for my affections and it's been an issue for all three of us the past month or so. Once he has the car in gear, he briefly glances in my direction. "You know, Tee, you juggling me plus these other guys was kind of funny for awhile, but it's not so funny any more. If you've got something going with Lenny—"

"I don't!" I am so aghast at the idea that Joe could even think I'd choose a romantic relationship with Lenny over one with him, I almost can't speak. "I'm not attracted to him like that." *At least I don't think I am.*

"Good."

"But he is a friend and I do care about him. He's in the hospital. He was in an accident last night."

"Is he all right? What happened?"

"I don't know exactly. He was on Everglades Boulevard and he flipped his truck. I saw his parents in the emergency room last night and his dad said he's banged up but he's going to be okay. I promised to stop and see him today, but I didn't get off work until four, and if we don't go now, visiting hours will be over by the time we finish dinner."

I don't realize I almost sound like I'm pleading with him, laying out my case until Joe glances over at me. "It's okay, Tee. We'll go see Lenny."

The next time we stop at a stoplight I lean over and kiss him on the cheek. He gives me a questioning look. "Thank you," I say.

He grins. "Welcome."

A minute later he says, "You're still my date for the club's grand opening party, right? My *exclusive date.*"

"Of course." Joe's been talking about this party for weeks. As Heritage Bay Country Club's executive director, it is a very big deal for him.

I'm not only flattered that he invited me, I'm actually looking forward to it.

When we walk into Lenny's hospital room, his eyes light up when he sees me. They dim a little bit when he realizes I'm not alone. "Hi, Tee. Joe."

"I hope the other guy looks worse," Joe jokes.

"Oh, my God. Lenny." Lenny's face is swollen, he has a bunch of cuts and scrapes on every visible bit of skin I can see, which is from the neck up and his arms because everything else is covered by a hospital gown or the sheet. I take his hand and rub my thumb over the back of it. I didn't know how else to offer comfort. Especially if this is my fault.

"Aww, it's not as bad as it looks. Although I do have the mother of all headaches." He turns his head and shows us a swollen bump.

Movement from the visitors chair on the other side of the bed distracts me and I glance in that direction. A female creature unfolds herself and stares at us from kohl-lined eyes Lenny says, "Guys, this is Lily. This is Tee and Joe." We murmur greetings to each other. I can't stop staring at Lily. She is a cross somewhere between Goth and thrift store poster child. I don't know where to look. Her hair is dyed an unrelenting and unnatural black and cut in a severe style with straight bangs that dip below her eyebrows and harsh angles everywhere else. She has on a variety of mismatched jewelry, a faded Grateful Dead tee shirt and a truly dreadful pair of baggy black jeans. Looking at her I feel the same way I used to feel when I saw Lenny. There is just too much going on which makes it hard to focus on any one feature.

Lily mumbles something which sounds like, "I'll be back," and shuffles out of the room.

Whether Joe senses I want a few minutes alone with Lenny or he really does have to make a phone call, he tells me he'll wait for me at the hospital entrance.

He shakes hands with Lenny. "Take care of yourself."

As soon as Joe leaves, Lenny's eyes light up again. "Thanks for coming to see me."

I want to smack him. He so obviously has a thing for me. I wish he'd be a little more subtle because I really don't know how to deal with his feelings. I rest one hip on the edge of the bed. "Lenny, what happened? Was there another car?"

His eyes dim and he looks away, his jaw locked. "Yes."

"Was it them?" I ask softly. "The Albanians?"

"I don't know. It might have been."

"But why? You haven't done anything. Not since that night we followed them after the party.

They already came after me to warn me away. Why go after you now?"

Lenny gives me a pained look and my heart sinks. "Oh, God, Lenny. What did you do?"

"Nothing, really. Except dig through the property records to find out who owns that duplex we followed them to."

"Oh, Lenny, why?" I groan. "Why would you do that?"

His chin juts out determinedly. "If you must know, I did it to help you. Because I thought you wanted to get more information on them, find out what they were up to."

"I do, but..." I bite my lip. I reach out and feather my fingers through his hair. "I couldn't stand it if something happened to you. If they hurt you because of me." I can feel those damn tears well in my eyes. Who would I to lose next? Who would be hurt because I couldn't leave this thing with the Espresso Mafia alone? Joe?

I have to look away because something springs up between me and Lenny the moment I touch him and I know he senses it, too. I don't want to encourage him.

"I also didn't like what was going on at my dad's birthday party. Those girls." Lenny stares at me.

At Steve Shutzel's birthday party we discovered that at least one of the young women posing as a member of the catering staff was actually servicing some of the male guests behind a locked bedroom door. Steve Shutzel included. At first Lenny was appalled, then embarrassed and then downright angry about what was going on. We'd followed the same silver Toyota we'd seen one of the Espresso Mafia driving before to an address in Silvergate. During my time as a cockroach, I'd infiltrated a dwelling which appeared to house the woman at the party as well as several others. I hadn't seen the outside of the place, but I assumed it was the same location. Lenny had gone a step further, digging into the ownership records of that duplex on his own.

"Lenny, I want you to stop. Stop doing research, stop looking up property records, stop following them."

"Want to know who owns that property?" Lenny needles.

Lenny knows I do. But I don't want the information if the price of having it is Lenny's life. "No. It's too dangerous—"

"A guy named Nicolai Arian Strakosha."

I cover my ears.

"Want to know what else he owns?" Lenny goes on as if I haven't reacted at all. "A bunch of stuff around town, restaurants mostly—"

He breaks off and shifts his gaze over my shoulder. I turn around to see Lily glowering at us. Or maybe that's her normal expression. She pauses inside the door.

I slide off the bed. "I have to go. Joe's waiting." I bend and touch my cheek to Lenny's. That was the wrong thing to do. He turns and grazes my cheek with his lips. When I straighten he has a devilish glint in his eye.

"Behave yourself," I hiss. "And don't do anything else."

I nod to Lily and escape.

Joe is waiting right where he said he'd be and he doesn't seem perturbed at how long I made him wait. We arrive at a seafood restaurant overlooking the bay where I proceed to be the worst date Joe has probably ever had. I'm tired and distracted and somehow I've lost my appetite.

"I pick at the expensive meal and feign interest in Joe's conversational attempts, until he finally gives up.

I reach across the table and cover his hand with mine. "I'm sorry. I'm terrible company."

He doesn't disagree.

"I'll make it up to you," I promise wondering how I'm going to do that.

He grins. "You will? That gives me something to look forward to. Do you want to take that home?" He indicates my nearly full plate. "You might be hungry later."

I let the server place most of my meal in a styrofoam box. We are quiet on the drive back to my place. I am in need of some serious sleep. At my door, Joe kisses me quite thoroughly and I know what I can do to pay him back. Not tonight, but sometime soon.

He doesn't seem in any hurry to move our relationship to the next level. All we've done since we've been going out is kiss. I'm fine with going slow, but now I wonder what Joe's deal is. Most guys in his situation would expect an overnight stay by the third date. He hasn't even attempted second base. Maybe he isn't as attracted to me as he pretends to be. Which doesn't explain why he keeps asking me out.

Magic makes a brief appearance after Joe leaves, lifting his nose into the air and eyeing the container from the restaurant before I set it in the refrigerator. "Nothing for you sour puss," I tell him, knowing the portion of red snapper I haven't eaten will probably end up in his food bowl sometime tomorrow. He acts like he could care less, turns his back on me and stalks away.

⁇

Chapter Six

I will heap evils upon them

"Is this irritating your eyes?" The girl at the Lancome counter stops swiping mauve eye shadow on my lids and peers at me closely.

"No, why?"

She gives a little shrug. "Your eyes look a little swollen or something." She glances at Sammi for confirmation.

Sammi peers at me oddly. "There is something going on with your eyes, Tee. You look a little, I don't know, bug-eyed?"

Bug-eyed? I've had a few too many experiences of temporarily being a bug recently not to panic a little. I turn to look in the mirror on the counter and stare at my reflection. The cosmetic counters in Macy's are pretty well lit and I can easily see my eyeballs look abnormal. They are larger than they used to be and quite round, bulging out past my eyelids. Bug-eyed? Or frog-eyed?

I turn a bit to try to see how bad they're bulging and catch a glimpse of something else. *What's that*? I touch my temple with my fingers. My skin has an odd, scaly texture and I think I notice a hint of green. Horrified, I stroke the patch of skin and as I do I notice something else. The ends of my fingers have started to pucker. I stare at my hands. Sure enough, there are indentations at the ends of each of my fingers, almost like they're forming small suction cups. *Like a tree frog...*

My mind rebels at the thought, the very idea and I can't hold back my moan of despair. "Oh, noooo." Quickly I look down at my feet. I am wearing flipflops so as nonchalantly as I can, I study the tips of my toes. Even from my seated position I can see that like my fingers, they are indented and beginning to look suction-cuppy.

I think my brain might explode. I am turning back into a frog. Or at least exhibiting physical characteristics of the creature I'd transformed into last. What if I do? What if I turn into a human tree frog? Lose all my hair and my skin and instead have that sort of slick, slimy green covering? My hands won't be hands any more but pads with extensions and suction cups. I'll have these big bulgy eyes. I'll have to stick close to damp areas or I'll dry up and blow away. On the upside, there will be no more bad hair days.

I swore I wouldn't swallow another bean and I haven't. I want to. Desperately. But I've resisted so far. It has been eight days since I swallowed one, turned into a frog and witnessed things I had no desire to. Marco, Sammi and Dr. Parker.

I've been normal these past few days. I caught up on my sleep. Lenny got out of the hospital and we'd had a couple of text message sessions, although I haven't seen him. He'd been advised to take it easy for a few more days and he was staying with his parents in Pointe Royale. Cody and I had called a truce. I cooked him spaghetti and afterward we went to Pelican Harry's and met up with Lexie and Matt and Erin and a few of the others in our crowd. We played pool and drank beer and it was almost like it used to be between us.

But if I turn into a human frog, that will pretty much change life as I know it. Maybe I won't even stay human. Maybe I'll lose my whole self. I'll shrink into a frog body, live out my life, which I expect will be rather short, die and no one will know what happened to me. I'll basically disappear.

Except what if it takes a long time for me to metamorphose into a complete frog? And in the meantime I just get scalier, and greener and more bug-eyed? I'll be a freak.

"Tee? You okay?" Sammi touches my shoulder.

I jolt out of my horrified reverie. "Yeah, I'm fine."

I look in the mirror again and finger-comb my hair over my temples to cover up the scales. "I think maybe I am having a reaction to this make-up. I'll just go to the restroom and wash it off, okay?" I give the make-up girl a pathetic smile which she returns.

"We have an excellent eye make-up remover in this same line. Let me just get some cotton balls—"

"No!" She and Sammi stare at me. I lower my voice. "That is, I think I'd better use plain old soap and water." I slide off the stool. "Sammi, I'll meet you in the shoe department, okay?"

"Want me to go with you?"

"No, it's okay. I'll be right back."

The last thing I want Sammi to notice is that I'm turning green. Bad enough she's seen my bulging eyes. In the restroom I check myself over as best I can without stripping down in front of the mirror and chancing that other shoppers will get more than they bargained for if they walk in on me. So far all I notice is the eyes, the bit of scaliness on my temple and my suction-cup fingers and toes.

I wash the eye shadow off and thoroughly wash my hands from habit, feeling my fingers get even more suctiony when the water hit them.

Note to self: Stay away from water. Speeds up transformation.

I have the shakes when I walk out the restroom. I'm a freak, more of a freak than I've ever been. I always felt like I didn't quite fit in with the rest of the human race even before I'd swallowed one of those damn forbidden beans. But now? I'd give everything I had to go back to being my normal misfit of a human self. Except I'm afraid I'm never going to be able to.

This is supposed to be my day out with my sister. I want to enjoy our time together and be supportive in case she wants to open up to me. Instead, our outing is turning into my own personal nightmare.

My thoughts careen around in my head as I make my way to the shoe department. This is the longest I've ever gone without swallowing a bean. After that first one, I hadn't been able to resist them for more than a few days. I hadn't even tried to resist them before I figured out they were what caused my transformations. Even then, the lure of them had been too much for me. I hadn't really regretted turning into any of the previous entities because ultimately I'd been able to do justice to Randall Grimes. It's only now, when my experience hit too close to home that I've begun to seriously resist my craving for just one more bean.

Apparently these are my choices: Swallow a bean and continue the transformations. Don't swallow a bean and turn into a frog.

Definitely a no-brainer. I'll have to get into the storeroom at work soon and access the bag of beans again.

I can only hope consuming a bean will rid me of the tree-frog symptoms I'm currently experiencing. If it doesn't, I am up the proverbial creek without a paddle.

I have one problem, however. I'm not scheduled to work again until the day after tomorrow.

Sammi sees me coming toward her. I can tell by her expression things are not good. "I think it got worse. Maybe we should go."

This is why I love my sister. I never have to be the bad guy with her. She has a way of bailing me out before I dump on her.

"I think you're right. I'm not feeling so hot."

"Poor, Tee." She steers me toward the exit. "I never knew you had such sensitive skin. Is this why you avoid wearing make-up?"

I really, really don't want to lie any more than I absolutely have to. "Partly," I reply.

"Will you be okay driving?" Sammi asks worriedly when we reach my Jeep. "Your eyes really look terrible."

"I can see okay, though," I assure her. I can't have her at my place, hovering, while my transformation continues to progress. "I'll be fine. I'll put a cool cloth on my eyes when I get home. I'm sure that will help." Shit. I lied again. I don't think anything is going to help. Except swallowing one of those forbidden coffee beans.

Sammi doesn't look convinced but she doesn't push it. "Okay. I'll call you later." She hugs me and starts off to where her car is parked.

I drive home as quickly as I can and get into my apartment without seeing anyone else. In the bathroom I strip down and search for more signs of froggishness. The scaly place on my face has increased. I'm sure it's tinged with green. My eyes seemed to have stopped bugging out, but they are so round my eyelids barely close over them.

My fingers and toes are more suction-cuppy. I'm dying of thirst. I get a big glass of ice water and run tepid water in the bathtub. I hunker down in there for awhile with a wet washcloth over my eyes. I begin to feel more comfortable. Of course. I'm doing what comes naturally.

To a frog.

Eventually I get out of the tub and wrap myself in a towel and get in bed to contemplate my options. I wake in an odd position, on my tummy with my arms and legs tucked up under me. *Like a frog!*

What the hell am I going to do? I'm off work tonight, tomorrow and tomorrow night. Who knows what I'll look like Monday morning? Will I be hopping in to work? Easily lifting pitchers and milk jugs with my suction cup fingers? How green will I be by then?

Back in the bathroom I stare at my reflection. I definitely have frog eyes. I stick out my tongue. What the hell? It looks longer and narrower than it usually does. Doesn't it? Not like I examine my tongue a whole lot. How frustrating to not have anyone else to ask about this. I can imagine seeing if Cody will come over. "I'm afraid I'm turning into a frog. What do you think?" That will probably push Cody over the edge. He'll decide for sure I'm certifiable and suggest a nice long stay in the county mental health facility. I can hear his explanation to my family and Dr. Parker. "She thinks she's a frog." By then, I won't just think I'm a frog. I'll probably be one.

Since Sammi and I didn't have lunch as we'd planned I wander out to the kitchen and peruse the contents of my refrigerator. Something cold. And green. Like I will be soon.

I put together a salad and sprinkle it with raisins and dried cranberries and some nuts. I am tempted to zap my tongue out and practice picking up the raisins one at a time. My whole mouth feel weird and sticky. I drink more water and start nibble my salad. I'll probably lose my teeth, I think glumly. Frogs don't have teeth. I'll grow a tailbone or something.

Magic strolls by the table and stops to stare and sniff the air without getting too close. Do I smell like a frog? What do frogs smell like anyway if they even smell? I sniff my arm, which is when I notice another patch of scaly skin with a slight green tinge. Uh-oh. There is some on my other arm, too, and on my knees. Crap! What am I going to do?

I double-check my work schedule. If I wait until I'm scheduled for a shift, at the rate I'm going, I'll be completely scaly and green when I walked in the door of Java Jake's.

If the beans cause the transformations in the first place, surely the lack of them are also responsible for my current state. I hope to God swallowing another one will reverse this metamorphosis, because if not, I am doomed. I'll turn into a human frog. I'll have to quit my job at

Java Jake's, but I can get work on the carnival freak show circuit.

I'd seen a television show about a guy who had various kinds of surgery and implants and tattoos to make himself look like a human lizard. I can't imagine why anyone would want to go through life not at least resembling the human they'd been born to be. At the moment, all I want is to be messed up, misfit me.

I can't just walk into Java Jake's when I'm not scheduled to be there and go into the storeroom. I don't want anyone to see me in my current transformative state. My only option is to sneak in after the store closes tonight. Get to the beans, swallow one, and hope it reverses the symptoms so by the time I have to work I'm back to normal.

With my plan in place I go back to my salad. Just for fun I try picking up the raisins with my tongue. I have to hold the bowl close to my mouth, but I'm able to zap the raisins with rather impressive pinpoint precision. I wish they were crunchier. After I get all the raisins I do the same with the cranberries. Then I start to think about what other advantages there could be to having a long, narrow, sticky tongue. I think about kissing Joe with it. What if I can't control it and my tongue won't let go of his? Or if I run my suction-cup fingers through his hair and end up pulling out tufts of it? Definitely I'll have to avoid Joe until I'm back to what passes as normal for me.

I'll have to lay low for the rest of the day. I decide to clean my apartment and do laundry, both tasks I tend to neglect until they absolutely have to be done. Joe calls in the evening to see if I want to go grab a bite somewhere. I tell him I can't because I went shopping with Sammi and tried some new makeup and am having a reaction to something. Everything I say is true and I'm pretty proud of the fact that I didn't lie to Joe. I've learned to let people in my life draw their own conclusions about what I tell them. It is so much easier than lying.

After talking to Joe I can't stop thinking about him. If swallowing a magic bean doesn't cure what ails me, I can kiss Joe goodbye. Permanently. With my long, sticky tongue.

I decide to wait until midnight before sneaking into Java Jake's. By then, the gym, the Presto supermarket, the nail salon and the drugstore will be closed. The dry cleaner, the sub shop and the shipping store will have closed much earlier and there shouldn't be anyone around the plaza.

I have a bad moment after I leave my apartment and hear one of the other tenants coming up the stairs. I take off at a run to the end of the building and another set of stairs that will take me to the parking lot. At least I can still run. I haven't been reduced to hopping yet.

My nerves are jangling by the time I get to the plaza parking lot. I drive around the entire plaza before I park at the far end of the row down from the Java Jake's entrance. There are only a few other cars in the parking lot. I don't pay much attention to them.

I'm wearing one of my black work shirts and black pants and sneakers. The very last thing I want is for anyone to see me. I have that sick humming feeling in the pit of my stomach. I stride purposefully to the Java Jake's door trying to act like I do this all the time, which I do. Just not at midnight and looking more and more like a frog with every passing minute.

I insert the key, twist it, step inside and lock the door behind me. There is enough light inside the store for me to see the alarm keypad. All I have to do is press in my four-digit code to turn the alarm system off. One. Two. Four. Eight. When I press the one key, the little suction cup that has developed on the end of my finger won't let go. I use my other hand to yank the end of my finger back and accidentally depress the one key a second time.

Shit!

Now I've screwed up the alarm code. I'd done this once before and I know what will happen. In a couple of minutes the alarm inside the store will begin an annoying periodic bleeping sound. Shortly afterward the phone will ring. On the other end will be someone from the alarm company. He'll ask me to identify myself, the store number and a bunch of other information to make sure I am who I say I am. If I don't answer the phone or if I give the wrong answer, he'll call the local cops and they'll come and make sure no one has broken in.

My heart hammers in panic while my thoughts race. Given everything I know about the local cops, in this case, the sheriff's department, they won't be overly concerned about an alarm going off at Java Jake's. Alarms go off all the time in south Florida, mostly due to the weather, or power surges, or some other malfunction. A tripped alarm will be low on the priority list. They'll get here when they get around to it.

I figure I have at least ten minutes before I have a problem on my hands and it won't take me even five to get into the storeroom, unearth my bag of beans, swallow one, put the beans back and get out. I'll be safely in my car and cruising for home by the time the cops show up.

In the morning, whoever is scheduled to open will know the alarm wasn't set. Initially the blame will fall to whoever closed last night. But there will be no sign of forced entry and nothing disturbed or taken so everyone will chalk the incident up to some sort of malfunction. Jerry will probably be notified and they'll get the alarm company out to check over the system. Not my problem.

I go in to the storeroom without turning on any lights. There is one left burning in the back room and with the storeroom door open I can see well enough. On my hands and knees I rearrange the items on the bottom shelf, reach to the back and pull out the forbidden beans. No time for my ritual of gazing down into the bag of sparkly-coated coffee beans; of withdrawing one and staring at it, of finally putting it into my mouth and sucking at the coating to see if I can figure out what it is I taste, why I am so addicted. None of that. I reach in, grab a bean, put it in my mouth and swallow.

The alarm begins its low-pitched repetitive beeping.

The phone on Jerry's desk begins to ring.

I roll the top of the bag down, shove it back into its hiding place behind the shelf, replace the jugs of white chocolate mocha and Frosty Coffee syrup and stand. I step out of the storeroom and close the door.

The phone stops ringing. The beeping continues. I cross the back room and stop for a moment at the end of the counter. Something is going on outside. I crouch down and peered around the edge of the counter. Two bright lights beam into the store from the outside. I duck back quickly before they spot me.

I hear the low murmur of male voices. Now I know what it means to be petrified. To be trapped. I have no idea who's out there. The lights are flashing in through the front windows to shine all around the store. Cops? How can they have responded so quickly?

I creep along behind the counter to the hand-off bar at the other end and peek over the opaque glass shield. I duck back behind the shield quickly as one of the lights sweeps over the glass. There are two deputies out there and a squad car with its red and blues twirling and its headlights aimed in the direction of the store entrance.

I can't get caught inside the store. For one thing, I can't explain why I'm here. For another, I can't explain my frog-like appearance. The most horrible thing I can imagine, beyond anyone else seeing me like this is that I'll be arrested and a mug shot will be taken. I'll be front page news in the Seagate Sentinel tomorrow: Frog Woman Breaks Into Local Business.

With their noses practically pressed up to the store's windows, those cops can surely hear the alarm.

I crouch and skedaddle to the backroom. If only my panicked brain could focus on one thought instead of six things at once. I happen to glance up to the bank of security cameras. There I am, if anyone ever cared to look at the footage. Someone certainly will if I leave evidence of my presence. I ease out of camera range, around the shelves and past the sinks and dish sanitizer. To my left is the storeroom door. To my right is the back door. I can escape out the back door! No one will see me. The same key that opens the front door unlocks the back. All I have to do is insert my key, turn it, release the deadbolt and push on the emergency exit handle. Once I'm through the door, I can retrieve my key and let the door fall closed. It will automatically lock. As far as I know no one has a key to unlock it from the outside. The only thing out of place will be the deadbolt in the unlocked position, but I don't count this as critical. Occasionally someone forgets to flip the deadbolt back into the locked position from the inside. Once closed the door can't be opened from the outside anyway. But if anyone tries to get out without using a key, the emergency exit handle will set off an alarm.

Without thinking twice I dig the key out of my pocket, insert it and turn it, flip back the deadbolt, push on the handle and open the door. I yank my key out, pocket it and let the door fall closed behind me. Now what?

My Jeep is in the front lot. I'll have to circle the plaza on foot to get to it, but I sure as hell can't attempt that until I'm sure the cops have left the area. No sooner do I have this thought, than a patrol car streaks across the parking lot, lights twirling but no siren. I duck behind one of the oversized recycling bins, although there is no need.

I know where I can hide, though, until the cop activity dies down. Just beyond the parking and delivery area behind the plaza is one of several man-made lakes connected to the adjacent golf course community. A line of trees provide a shield for the rather unsightly rear of the plaza with its loading docks and dumpsters. There are several small lakes throughout the development which attract ducks and other water fowl. Frogs probably, too, I think as I duck and run across the pavement. Just as I reach the curb another patrol car turns into the parking lot tires screeching, lights twirling but again no siren. I dive into the cover of the trees blindly, stumbling across the narrow bank. Unable to stop my momentum I fall face first into the lake.

I inhale and swallow some truly disgusting and I know for a fact, non-potable water, before I manage to right myself. I cough and gag and fight my way back to the bank. The mud on the bottom sucks so hard at my shoes that I lose one.

I sit down hard on the narrow bank and swipe at my face with my hands. I wish I had something to dry myself with because I am soaked. Gag me. What a mess. Maybe I should just stay here, join the other frogs which are sure to be about and live out my frogly existence until it comes to its natural conclusion.

I hope I don't catch any dread disease. The golf course uses reclaimed sewage water for irrigation. Any excess drained into the lakes along with the runoff from fertilizer and insecticide. None of which seems to have any ill effect on the ducks or the occasional otter or alligator. I can only hope I'll be as lucky.

I don't know how long I sit on the bank. Long enough to realize I'm exhausted. My heart rate has slowed to normal and I almost don't care if I get caught. At least I can take a nap in jail. They'll give me a dry orange jumpsuit. A baloney sandwich maybe. No more cop cars cut through the parking lot behind me. I can hear the swoosh of occasional traffic along Pine Ridge Road, and the hum of the plaza's air conditioning equipment but other than that it's pretty quiet.

When I stand rivulets of water dribble to the ground or collect in my remaining shoe. I toe it off, bummed to have lost one of my sneakers. Something else to add to my shopping list.

Just in case the cops are still lurking about, I decide to stick close to the trees. They'll provide cover until I reach the end of the plaza behind the drug store. There are enough bushes in the landscaping along Merlot Way to cover me until I get close to the front of the plaza. From there I should be able to see what's going on, if anything, and determine whether I can get back to the Jeep without detection.

I pick up my sodden shoe and begin to pick my way through the trees along the narrow bank. Every time I take a step, leaves and grime and small twigs stick to my wet socks, poking me and forcing me to go slow. The last thing I want is to lose my footing and take another tumble into the water. There are only four or five feet between the curb and the water's edge with gaps between the cover of trees and tangle of bushes. There is just enough light from the back of the plaza and the streetlights on the far side of the lake to allow me to see where I'm going. I try to be quiet but I squish, squish, squish my way along nonetheless.

At the far end of the lake I pause and listen and peer through the fringe of leaves. I don't see or hear anything out of the ordinary. On the other side of Merlot Way, the lights of the hospital shine. I dash across the pavement and duck behind a bunch of hibiscus bushes, stop and listen and look around some more. Still nothing.

I race past the drug store's drive-up window lanes and crouch near the bike rack tucked into a corner just behind the plaza walkway. More hibiscus bushes hide me from view.

On the corner of the plaza property where Merlot Way intersects Pine Ridge, is the gas station with the McDonald's. It is ablaze with light. There is one car at the pumps. The McDonald's is closed. I can see minimal activity inside. The building is situated far enough away from where I am that it doesn't present a problem. I have to risk being out in the open, though, to get to the Jeep from here. My best bet is to hustle from one parking median to the next where again, there are at a least a few trees and bushes, though much sparser, that will give me a bit of cover.

I make a dash for the nearest median and stop near a tree for a second before racing across the empty blacktop to the next one. I keep this up, moving diagonally each time so I'll end up closer to where I left the Jeep.

The closer I draw to my goal, however, the more dismayed I become. There is a car parked in the angled space facing the Jeep.

At the final median I hide as best I can behind the trunk of a palm tree and study the situation. It's impossible to tell if there is anyone in the other vehicle. I don't see any movement. But if the car's driver could park anywhere in the lot, why park across from me?

I stare hard at the car, a non-descript dark gray, late-model sedan. The adrenaline that kept me going until now is gone. I want only to get to the Jeep, get home, get into my apartment without being noticed, get out of my disgusting wet clothes and into a hot shower and from there into bed. But I'm afraid to approach the Jeep.

I wait but nothing happens. No patrol cars. Is that sedan an unmarked cop car waiting for me to return to the Jeep? Did they "make" me? Did they somehow know that it was me who triggered the alarm in Java Jake's? How could I explain my furtive presence there if they checked the security footage? I'd have to figure something out if it came to that.

If I'd been thinking clearer, if I was smarter, I would have waited and answered the phone when the alarm company called. I knew the passwords, knew how to identify myself to them. I could have explained that I'd accidentally hit the wrong number on the keypad and that would have been the end of that.

Screw it, I think once again. I head for the Jeep with my key poised to unlock the door. I am ready to insert my key when the sedan's headlights come on and the driver's side door opens.

Panic shoots through me. I instinctively glance at the individual exiting the vehicle at the same time the keys fall out of my shaking hand and my mouth drops open. I stare in shock as he approaches. "Father Tom?"

There are a lot of regular Java Jake's customers I like. A few I absolutely loathe. And even fewer I can honestly say I love. Father Thomas Murphy is one of those few. I'm not a hundred percent sure what his deal is. About a year ago we got to talking one day when I was on my break and we sort of struck up a friendship from there. Here's what I know about Father Tom: He's a Catholic priest who operates some kind of halfway house on the outskirts of Seagate. My impression is the house is a place for a variety of society's dregs.

Homeless, recovering addicts, prostitutes trying to get out of the business, runaways. There are rumors that Father Tom also harbors individuals who are in the country illegally from time to time when the Immigration Service starts breathing down their necks, but I don't know if that's fact or fiction.

What I do know, from the occasional newspaper articles about him and from the little that Father Tom himself has shared is that the Catholic Church frowns on Father Tom's activities, but that's he's such a successful fundraiser, they have no choice but to keep him in the fold. He's affiliated with one of the local parishes, but most of the time he's at the halfway house which operates under the name Eagle's Wings. Father Tom told me he took the name from a line in his favorite hymn.

Father Tom doesn't look like a priest, that's for sure. He's probably in his mid-forties. His hair is kind of long and unkempt. There are a few gray streaks but most of it is a medium brown shade. He's got a decent body for a guy his age in that he doesn't have a beer gut or anything. Mostly when I see him he's wearing jeans or baggy cargo shorts and tee shirts and flipflops. Once in a while he'll stop in after he's said Mass somewhere and he'll have on that black uniform with the white collar that priests wear out in public. Not that I'm into him that way or anything, but when he shows up in priest clothes, he's pretty handsome.

I like talking to him. His eyes light up whenever he's engaged in conversation. He can make you feel like you're the most important person in the world and whatever you're saying he's finding absolutely fascinating. He *listens*. He's got this philosophical way of viewing things, but he's never judgmental.

"Tee. Are you all right?" He slips between the front ends of our cars and comes toward me. He looks at me curiously and that's when I remember my hideous appearance. I throw my hands up to cover my frog face.

"No. Don't look at me."

"Tee. What's wrong? Are you hurt?" He gently pries my hands away from my face.

"Please. I'm hideous," I blubber, as the events of the past twenty-four hours engulf me.

Father Tom chuckles. "You're hardly hideous, Tee. You look to me just like you always do. Except you're wet and a bit muddy."

"I am?" I move so I can look in the Jeep's side mirror. The headlights of Father Tom's sedan shine brightly in my face. Swallowing the bean worked! My frog face has disappeared. I'm me again. "Oh, thank God." I am so relieved I nearly swoon. I slump against the Jeep's door. Father Tom stoops and retrieves my keys. I let them dangle from the ends of my no longer suction-cup fingers.

"I'm glad to see that you're all right," Father Tom says after a bit.

"Father Tom, what are you doing here?"

"Ah. One of the less pleasant aspects of my job and my lack of popularity with the local church hierarchy is that when there's an emergency call in the middle of the night, it's directed my way. I had to perform Last Rites at the hospice facility and afterward I stopped for gas." He nodded in the direction of the gas station. "Apparently, it was been robbed at gunpoint right before I arrived and the thief escaped on foot. Next thing I know the place is swarming with patrol cars and deputies."

"Oh."

"I cut through the parking lot on my way out and I saw your Jeep and I thought, well, I don't really know what I thought. That perhaps you and the thief had crossed paths; that he'd prevented you from returning to your car. I decided to wait a bit."

"Oh."

My tired brain wouldn't process very well. I now felt quite safe from detection by the sheriff's department or anyone connected to Java Jake's. Not only had no one seen me enter or leave the store, they weren't looking for me to begin with. As far as the tripped alarm, they could have checked it out. Jerry could have shown up during the time I was drip-drying, discovered nothing amiss and returned home. As long as no one checked the security camera footage I was safe.

"You're all right, then, Tee? Not injured or anything?"

"I'm fine."

Father Tom looks at me curiously but doesn't question me further. "Will you be all right going home, or wherever you're going?"

"Yes. Of course."

"I'll say good-night, then. Take care, Tee."

"Goodnight, Father."

He starts back to his car.

"Father?"

He stops and turns to look at me.

"Could you maybe say a prayer for me? I think I'm going to need it."

He smiles. "You don't even need to ask, Tee. You're always in my prayers." He pauses a beat before he says, "And Tee, if you ever need someone to talk to, or anything else, my door's always open."

He waves and gets in his car. I don't know why but hearing him say that he prays for me gives me a sense of comfort I didn't have before. I get into the Jeep hating the fact that I'm dirty and wet and every bit of the ick is going to seep into the driver's seat. I need to keep some beach towels in the back in case I need them because this is the second time in the last several weeks that I've been covered in ick and I've had to drive home. I shudder at the memory of my dumpster-diving adventure where I'd wound up covered in fish guts.

I put the Jeep in gear and drive home without incident. I drag my sorry ass up the stairs and almost make it into my apartment undetected. Except Cody's door pops open and he assesses me from head to toe. Cody's apartment faces the parking lot and I happen to know that he has no qualms about keeping tabs on the tenants. Including me. Even in the wee hours of the morning. I always liked that he was looking out for all of us and watching over us so to speak. At the moment not so much.

"What happened to you?"

No need to lie. "I fell into a lake."

He looks me over some more. He wants to interrogate me further I can tell. "Do I want to know?" he asks.

I almost collapse in gratitude at his question. "No. No, you really don't."

"You okay?"

"Yeah."

"Okay. I'll see you later."

He waits while I unlock my door and go inside before his door closes softly.

Chapter Seven

My enemies will boast

I wake up late the next morning ridiculously grateful to be myself. I stare at my reflection in the bathroom mirror and am pleased to see no signs of greenish scales or bulging eyes.

Even knowing that I will temporarily turn into something else before the day is over doesn't take away from my feeling of contentment. I understand now, the power of the forbidden beans. If I fight my addiction I'll turn into a human form of whatever I was last.

I don't ever want to risk not having access to the beans if I need one. I'll have to remove a few and keep them with me at all times for emergency purposes only. I can do that when I go in for my shift later today. I should keep a calendar too and track my bean consumption. I need to exert as much control over the power of the beans as possible.

I count back the days to the one when I'd turned into a tree frog and seen Sammi cutting herself. Then counted forward to when I'd begun to exhibit symptoms of tree froggedness. Eight days. Counting yesterday, I'd gone nine days without a bean and the consequences had been most unpleasant. I can't go longer than seven days without risking the same sort of experience I just went through. I have to have a bean a week.

By midnight tonight I'll experience at least one transformation. I hope it happens while I'm at work, because that actually seems to work in my favor. I'm able to function at my job and I'm more pleasant when only part of me occupies my body. Maybe I'll get a raise.

The downside of temporarily transforming during the day is I have no memory of what happens to me as a human during that time.

But since I am completely human for the moment I will put my physical fitness plan into action. I don a tee shirt, shorts and sneakers. After a healthy breakfast of blackberry yogurt liberally laced with granola and of course, coffee, I drive to North Seagate Beach. I park near the boardwalk because I can run along it and enjoy the shade provided by the mangroves before I get to the beach.

I lock the Jeep and start off at a slow jog. I don't want to overdue and pull a muscle or something my first day out. I know it will take me awhile to build up my endurance so I alternate periods of running with walking. I check the time. I figure an hour for my first workout will be ideal.

The boardwalk is three quarters of a mile long and ends at an open area maintained by the county parks department. There are restrooms and a snack bar and a shop that sells sunscreen and floats and beach toys. Nearby is a hut where beach goers can rent chairs and cabanas and kayaks.

This time of year and this time of day the place is practically deserted except for the workers. The snack bar isn't open yet and no one is buying sunscreen.

I head north along the beach because I know there is a pass about a mile away which will be a good turning around point. I settle into a comfortable pace surprised to find I don't get as out of breath as quickly as I thought I would.

I decide I will schedule my runs around work. On my days off and the days I close there is no reason I can't run in the morning. I'll also check into pricing at the gym near Java Jake's and see if I can afford to join.

I hum a little tune as I jog along on the packed sand near the shore. Something about the beach makes it easier to think. The sun, the breeze, the water lapping at the shore calms me and lets me organize my thoughts.

Next I'll go gun shopping. I need to talk to Lenny and tell him to cease and desist researching the Albanians. After he shares what he's already found out, of course.

Lenny was an unexpected ally. He was really a good guy and even though sometimes I feel I'm using him, I'm glad he's in my life.

It is literally pouring down rain. I am on the inside edge of a sidewalk huddled up against a building. All I can see is concrete and beyond that the pouring rain, a bit of landscaping and a parking lot. It isn't cold, but I don't like being out here and I feel incredibly small. There's a crevice between the edge of the concrete and the building and I've wedged myself into it a bit. I feel pretty safe, yet vulnerable at the same time. Like anyone could come along and stomp on me and that would be it. Although they'll have to get the side of their foot at the exact right angle to get me.

I move forward a little bit and immediately know I have four legs. I look at my toes...feet...hands, whatever they are. Four...extensions I guess you'd call them. It's so hard to tell in the animal kingdom. Do creatures such as myself technically have feet or are what I think of as feet simply extensions of legs? From what I can see I am a sort of a grayish-brown. I've seen feet like mine many times. You don't grow up in south Florida like I did and never see a lizard. That's what we call them, anyway. They probably aren't technically lizards, but a member of the lizard family. Geckos, maybe or Anoles are the right term. Chameleons. They come in a variety of colors and sizes, I believe, but most of the ones I see are the color I am now. Grayish brown. Although I have seen green ones and ones with darker markings than I apparently have.

A car pulls into a nearby space. Its headlights shine right above me almost blinding me for a moment before they go out and the engine turns off. I hear a car door open and close and steps splashing through the puddled rain. Feet encased in black mens' shoes cross the sidewalk right in front of me.

The feet stop and I hear a jangle of keys, metal against metal and I perk up. There's a door a few inches away from me, above and to the right that I didn't know was there. He unlocks it and the door swings inward. The moment he steps inside, like a lightning bolt I skitter after him before the door swings shut.

It's dark inside and it takes my vision a minute to adjust. It must be nighttime. The sidewalk was lit overhead, but the parking lot lay in relative darkness.

I hear a lamp switch click and a light comes on. I strain to look around. You'd be surprised how hard it is. Mostly what I can see is floor covered in flat gray/blue carpet. The edge of a bedspread. Some nondescript furniture, a nightstand, a small table, a couple of chairs.

I scramble across the floor, pleased by how quickly I can move. Beats hell out of the crawl-hop-walk I was forced to do as a tree frog. I climb up the leg of the desk and crouch between the phone and the base of the lamp that's now on. I can see much better from up here. I do a quick three-hundred-and-sixty-degree turn. I'm in a motel room. An inexpensive one based on the furnishings. The man has gone into the bathroom. I can hear toilet sounds and the splash of water from the sink. When he comes out, he unlocks a briefcase he apparently left on the bed and withdraws a laptop computer. Before he can set it down on the desk I skedaddle back down the leg. I have sticky pads on my feet that hold me on the vertical climbs, and I know he hasn't seen me. I'm in no danger.

He sets the laptop down and drops into the desk chair. I peek over the top edge of the desk and watch while he scrubs his hands over his face and back through his hair. I gasp in surprise because I recognize him. He looks tired and grim and something inside me wants to comfort him. To pat him on the shoulder and tell him it will be okay. Not that I have any idea what's got him looking so down.

He lifts the lid on the laptop and stares at the screen, probably waiting for it to boot up. After a bit he starts tapping keys, pausing, reading, tapping more keys. I crawl down the desk leg and around to the chair. It's so easy to climb up the leg to the back of the chair. The chair has a low back but I can't see anything. No unless I crawl up on his shoulder or something.

He's wearing a long-sleeved blue dress shirt with the sleeves rolled back almost to his elbows. I think for a moment. Marco wasn't even aware of me crawling up his back when I was a tree frog. Of course, his brain was mostly disengaged at the time, all of the blood having been sucked into his nether regions. But still, at the moment I weigh practically nothing. I bet if I'm extra sneaky and quiet I can make it the several inches to the collar of my father's shirt and get a peak at whatever he finds so fascinating on his laptop.

I reach out one of my...fingers, then my whole...hand, leg, foot, whatever it was called. The sticky pads might be a bit of an issue against the material, but I hope not. I decide to just do it. I get all four feet on the shirt and tip-toe up until I can touch the hair curling over his collar. He needs a haircut. Someone should tell him that. I touch one of the strands with my stretchy finger-like toes. I guess I know now where I got my untamable head of hair with its inconsistent array of curls and waves and cowlicks.

I creep up a little further so I can see the computer screen over his shoulder. He's reading a document of some sort, a report maybe, because there is a lot of text. I can't make out all the words, but it seems to be a surveillance report. To the left are dates and times and to the right are paragraphs listing names and activities.

What does my father do? Is he a private investigator? Has he been following someone? Or do others follow and send him reports like these to review?

The names are all foreign and most likely last names. He hits the page down key rapidly, scanning more than reading, so only a word here and there jumps out at me. *Warehouse. Shipment. Weapons. Drop. Cover. Legitimate. Organization.*

One name pops out at me. *Strakosha.* Where did I hear that name recently?

My father exits the document and brings up a site entitled: Millennium Project. He accesses a log-in screen and taps in letters and numbers and symbols so rapidly I can't follow them. Next thing I know he's in some sort of internal e-mail program. I see an e-mail address in the "From" box with a name that means nothing to me. But the URL attached to it, I had definitely heard of. *Interpol.*

He types in an address to send to and begin a message in the body of the screen. I can't keep up with how fast he types and it's hard to read from this distance. My mind begins to wander. Does my father work for Interpol? For something called the Millennium Project? Do Interpol agents work in the United States? I thought Interpol was based in Europe. Great Britain or somewhere. Not like you ever hear a lot about them unless it's in a movie or something. I'm not even sure what Interpol actually is. International police?

I remind myself I need to get a computer so I can look stuff like this up. I have to close again tomorrow but I can go to the library in the morning and do a little research. I can at least research Interpol. Maybe this Millennium Project. See what that's all about. I'll check out the name Strakosha, too, just for the heck of it.

Maybe by then I'll remember where I heard it before.

So distracted am I that I'm not prepared for my father to lean back and run his hands through his hair again. His thumb whacks me on the nose and I go flying. My sticky feet pads aren't going to do a thing for me now, because there is nowhere to land behind the chair except the floor.

When I land I get the wind knocked out of me. I lay there on my belly, stunned. I don't think I'm hurt. After a few seconds, I creep under the bed. Last thing I need is for good old dad to push the chair back and squish me without even realizing I exist.

There is one thing I want to do before I metamorphose back into my human self and I'm pretty sure I know how to do it. I skitter my way through the dust-covered carpet under the bed to reach the nightstand. I climb up and sure enough there is a small notepad and a pen with exactly the information I need.

Chapter Eight

Oh, that they could understand!

After work the next night I wait until after dark and I park my Jeep outside a Wendy's. I go in and order a cheeseburger and a Sprite to go and escape through the exit on the opposite side.

My noticeable, memorable yellow Jeep is becoming a problem. It is too easy to spot and the last thing I want is for anyone to spot me easily. Not my father, not anyone I know and not the Espresso Mafia, just in case they happen to be following me.

There are no *coincidences*. That thought had played through my head the past couple of days. Ever since Lenny's "accident." The way those two Mafia guys had led me on a wild goose chase to the middle of nowhere. Father Tom in the parking lot the other night.

I have business to conduct and I don't want anyone to know about it. I duck and bob my way on the route to the motel, darting between parked cars, taking the scenic route behind a strip plaza, sticking close to landscaping whenever possible. Thank God I live in a community where some sort of landscaping is required for every business entity. The county does its own thing on the medians and other public areas. There's no shortage of places to hide. Every time I pause, I wait and watch, looking for any vehicle cruising by, anyone on foot, a tail of any sort. I see nothing out of the ordinary. I have to consider the possibility that anyone tailing me is better at it than I am at spotting a tail, but I honestly don't think anyone is following me.

The Sea Lion motel faces U.S. 37, the main highway that runs through Seagate. Within Seagate proper, it is known as Tamarind Trail and depending on the location along the trail, property there can be considered an upscale address. The Sea Lion is on the eastern fringe just before the rather tattered edges of the city begin. Whoever owns the motel is trying valiantly to maintain a reputable front while some of the other businesses around it either sit empty or look decidedly seedy.

I circle the motel property. It's easy to do because it isn't a big place. The office is at one end of the building with an overhang extending out in front of it. The rooms are stacked one on top of the other in a long building designed by an architect with absolutely no imagination whatsoever. All I have to do is figure out which room I was in the other night.

I hide in the landscaping surrounding the motel's parking lot. There aren't many parked cars and even fewer lights on in the room windows. The neon sign in front of the motel has some of its gas missing so it reads Sea L. I hum *A Kiss From a Rose* under my breath.

I wish I'd had more time in my lizard-like state to get my bearings before I darted into the room on my father's heels. I'd have a better idea of which room is his. I hadn't had time to get a good look at his car, either. My perspective is completely different now. All I know for sure is that his room is on the ground floor. I wonder if I walk along the sidewalk I can figure out exactly where I'd been.

No cars have pulled in or out since I've been watching the place. No one has come out of any of the rooms. I scan the area while sucking up my Sprite. I can stroll nonchalantly along the walkway until I get close to the office, then turn around and stroll back. The way the office area is situated, I doubt the clerk inside will be able to see me, if he or she is even paying attention, which in a place like this, I doubt.

Decision made, I step out of my hiding place pretending I haven't a care in the world. I walk the length of the sidewalk, pivot and walk back, concentrating on the proximity of the doors to the parking lot and the landscaping. I make it back to my hiding place and am fairly certain my father has the room at the very end closest to me.

I lean against the trunk of a palm tree and dig the Wendy's bag out of my purse. I unwrap the burger and prepare to take a bite when a car turns into the parking lot and heads in my direction. I drop to my knees, lose my balance and land on my butt in damp mulch, dropping my cheeseburger in the process. My stomach growls in protest. The car's headlights sweeps over the bushes, blinding me for a second before they switch direction, shine briefly on the motel's exterior then go out.

I stare hard at the nondescript gray sedan. An American model a year or two old. The driver's door opens and my father steps out, briefcase in hand. He locks the car, unlocks the door to his room and disappears inside. My heart is racing and my palms start to sweat. *Daddy.*

Weird how I can turn into a little girl again just seeing him. I've longed for him my entire childhood. My entire life, actually, since I have barely any memories of him. All I have is that picture of the four of us. I don't know where he's been the last twenty-plus years or what he's been doing. I'd always thought he'd abandoned us. But during our conversation a few weeks ago, my mother told me he'd discreetly sent her money all those years, doing his best to support the family he'd left.

I can just barely make out the glow of light against the heavy draperies that cover the only window in the unit. I wondered if his routine is the same every night. Return to his room, visit the bathroom, set up his laptop on the desk and read and send reports. I am about to find out.

I wait another few minutes before I dash across the crumbling blacktop to his door. My nerves jangle and my stomach knots. Probably a good thing I dropped my burger or it'd be threatening to come up about now. Just as I raise my hand to knock, the door opens. Steely fingers wrap around my wrist and yank me inside.

The barrel of a gun presses against my head while the heavy metal door slams shut. I stop breathing. Seconds tick by, both of us frozen in that position, he with his fingers encircling my wrist so hard it hurts, pressing the barrel of the gun above my ear, me standing stock still in shock.

When he doesn't press the trigger I turn my head so I can look at him. I start to breathe again when the gun drops to his side.

"Tango." He stares at me, his eyes awash in so many emotions I can't begin to track them all. Fear. Frustration. Love. Anger, maybe?

"Daddy."

All the fight seems to go out of him when he hears me speak. He slumps a little as if I've just taken the gun and turned it on him. He tucks it away behind his back.

"You should not call me that."

"It's what I always call you. How I always think of you."

He gives me such a look of heartbreak, of despair, I can feel tears press into my eyes. I force them back. I am not a crybaby.

"You should not be here." He is warning me again, just as he had the other two times I saw him. But there is a hollow ring to his tone, as if he doesn't mean it.

"But I am here. You'll have to deal with it."

He does that thing I am beginning to think of as one of his tells. He scrubs his hands over his face and back through his hair. He seems baffled by my presence and yet not a hundred percent surprised that I am here.

He steps to the window and lifts the drapery a bit and stares out. At the desk he picks up a cell phone and stares at the display. His laptop is on the desk, but the lid is closed. Either he hasn't had time to open it or he closed it when he came to the door.

"You were probably followed." He sets the phone down.

"I don't think so."

"I didn't see your vehicle in the parking lot."

"That's because it's not there."

"Where is it?"

I barely know this man, my father. Maybe he loves me. Maybe he doesn't. Maybe he views me as one giant pain in his ass and he'd like to get rid of me. That wasn't going to happen if I had any say in it. Not now that I'd found him, or he'd found me after all these years. Whatever he thinks of me or about me, one thing I do know. I want his respect.

I set my purse on the table, thinking carefully about what I want to say. "Look, I'm not an idiot. Or not as much of one as I was a few weeks ago. I take precautions. I'm careful. I'm not an expert, but I'm as certain as I can be no one followed me here."

"Where's your vehicle?"

I sigh, pull a chair out from the table and drop into it facing him. "There's a Wendy's down the road. I left it there." I outline the route I'd taken and what I'd done, emphasizing the fact that I hadn't seen anyone in a car or on foot who appeared to be interested in my movements.

When I finish, he inclines his head in what might be approval. I hope it is. He assesses me for a minute before he speaks. "Next time you're trying to lose a tail, go into the restroom. Change clothes if you can or keep a hat and glasses with you. If you're wearing a jacket take it off. If you have one with you, put it on. Try to change your persona. A wig's not a bad idea for someone like you. Carry yourself differently. Walk faster or slower. Anything that makes them question whether it's you or someone else they've spotted. If you're on foot and a car's following you, cross the street and walk in the opposite direction. Especially if there's traffic. Look for a crowd. Restaurants are good. You can probably get right through one, through the kitchen and out the back before anyone stops you."

I incline my head as he had before, and gaze at him with approval. He hasn't exactly embraced my presence here, but he hasn't sent me away or rejected me, either. Nor did he talk down to me.

"How did you find me?"

It takes everything in me not to look away when I answer. "I can't tell you that."

His gaze narrows. "Are you working for them? Are they using you to get to me?"

"Them who? The Albanians? No! Of course not!" Respect, indeed! That he could even think I'd stoop so low. I stand, pick up my purse and take a couple of steps toward the door. "This was a mistake," I mutter in his direction.

He is on me before I get any further. Those strong fingers of his wrap around my arm just above the elbow. "Tango." His voice saying my name is like a caress. No one ever calls me Tango. I'd hated my name from the moment I'd been old enough to say it. But on his lips it sounds beautiful and special and I love it. I know, because my mother told me, that she and my father decided to name me and Sammi after their two favorite dances. Dancing is what brought my parents together and also what led to the disappearance of my father's younger sister.

"I had to know. Do not be insulted. I had to see your reaction. Do you understand?"

His English is impeccable but his speech pattern has a formal, slightly halting rhythm to it which can't cover the fact that it is a second language for him. I guess I can understand why he'd question my motives in coming here, especially when I can't tell him how I found him.

"I do," I whisper. I so desperately don't want to leave. I finally found him and I want every minute I can get with him.

"Come. Sit." He gestures toward the chair I'd just vacated. "Would you like coffee?" He indicates the tiny coffeemaker provided by the motel for its guests. "The coffee it is terrible, but it is all I have."

I smile. I can drown in gourmet coffee every day at Java Jake's if I want to. How ironic that coffee beans were what led me to my father in the first place. Now he's offering me a cup of substandard brew. "I'd love some." I smile, knowing the coffee ritual, if nothing else, will serve to stretch out our time together.

"Tell me about your life," he says, when the coffee is ready and we each have a Styrofoam cup of it cooling nearby.

"You know about my life. You've been keeping tabs."

He doesn't deny it. Just gives me a steady look.

"Why don't you tell me about *your* life?"

Something like regret passes over his expression. Again he shoves the fingers of one hand through his hair. He takes a sip of the coffee. I get the feeling I'm making Daddy uncomfortable. "I cannot."

"Nothing? You can't tell me anything about yourself? Not even if you have a wife? Another family?" No idea where that came from, except it's a personal question and it has nothing to do with whatever his work is.

He relaxes a little back into his chair and holds the Styrofoam cup with both hands, gazing at me over the top of it. "I learned a long time ago what happens when I have people in my life I care about. It is not good for them."

"It wasn't good for you, either, from what I know."

The incline of the head again in acknowledgment. "But to answer your question, no. I have no family."

"You have us."

"In blood only."

"It can be more." Somehow I keep my voice even, a statement of fact, instead of the pleading whine I hear inside my head.

"No. I would not endanger you. Not Samba. Not your mother."

"Mom's married."

"Yes."

"Sammi is—" Oops. I can't tell my father Sammi's secrets.

Can I?

"Samba is what?"

"Troubled." I decide that is the best word for it. It tells him everything and nothing at the same time.

"I am sorry to hear that."

I lift a shoulder, let it drop. "Yeah, well. What's the Millennium Project?"

He straightens. I'd caught him off guard. "I don't know what you're talking about."

Did I inherit my lying skills from him? "Yes, you do."

He gives me that baffled look again. Only this time it's coupled with consternation. "It is not something I can discuss."

Might as well go for broke. "Are you a cop of some sort?"

"No."

"An investigator?"

"I cannot tell you."

I take a sip of the coffee to stall for time while I think of another question. As he'd said it would be, the stuff he'd brewed was truly awful, so weak it had barely any flavor at all. It looks and tastes like brown water. "What can you tell me?"

"Nothing."

"Why did you show up after all these years to warn me away from the Albanians?"

"You needed to be warned."

"Why?"

"Because you don't know what you don't know about them."

He's the one fishing now. He has no idea what I know. "Maybe I do. Maybe I don't."

"They are dangerous people. I would not like to see you hurt by them. By your pursuit of them."

"Like you were?"

His turn to lift a shoulder and let it drop.

"Did anyone warn you?"

He gives a low grunt that's now quite a laugh. "Of course. I had many *warnings*.

"But you didn't listen."

"Not at first. Not at all, I suppose. I simply learned to be more careful."

"I'm learning to be careful, too."

"It would be better if you would learn to stay out of their business."

"I can't. I won't."

"I can't watch out for you."

"I'm not asking you to."

"Tango." In his voice there is a plea. His hand goes through his hair again.

"I can help you."

"No."

"I can find out things. We can work together."

"No."

"Why not?"

"I work alone."

"Me too." If he only knew how alone I am.

I have no idea what my father does and he won't tell me. I'd looked up Interpol on the internet at the library this morning. I was right. It was an international policing network based in Lyon, France. As near as I could determine its main function is to gather and share data about criminal activity on a worldwide basis. Like a law enforcement clearing house.

I'd also researched the Millennium Project, but I'd found very little information. It appeared to be a study jointly funded by Interpol and The United Nations to gather information about human trafficking. I wasn't certain of anything beyond that.

My father picks up his cell phone, taps his thumb on the screen, stares at it for a moment then sets it back on the desk. The phone itself hadn't made a sound.

"Why do you keep looking at your phone?"

With his chin he gestures toward the door. "Security camera feeds into it. I like to know who is outside."

That explained how he'd whipped the door open before I'd had a chance to knock.

"I found you," I point out. "I didn't lead anyone here. If I had a tail to begin with, and I don't think I did, I must have lost them, right?"

"I cannot argue with this."

"I'm not dumb. I can help you."

"Tango, it is not possible."

"What if I tell you what I know? Would you think about it?"

"You may tell me. It will change nothing."

"You feed on information about these guys. I would think you'd want to know everything you could no matter the source."

"Some sources are too dangerous. I find information other ways."

"I guess we're done here, then." I say it but make no move to get up and leave. I sit there and look at him while he looks at me.

"Tango, what is it you want? Why did you come here?"

A big knot works its way up from my stomach to my throat and threatens to choke me. Everything I feel and want, all the reasons I came here, roll into a big ball and get stuck inside me. I'm not sure I can explain to him how important he is to me. How important it is to me that he lets me help him nail the Espresso Mafia. I can hardly explain it to myself.

"I want..." Tears press against the backs of my eyes and I almost don't care if he sees them or if they fell. Not if it sways him to my side. "I never forgot you. I have that picture, the same one you have of the four of us on my nightstand. I always wondered why you left. I never quite bought the story Dorothea told us. I never believed you'd abandoned us or that if you did you didn't have a good reason. Now I know it's true."

A single tear slides over my bottom lid and I let it go, let it run down my cheek. I keep my gaze steady on his. He fists one hand and rests his chin on it while he listens.

"You came out of nowhere to warn me away from the Albanians so I know you must care a little."

He takes in an audible breath and I think he wants to say something then but he doesn't.

"I do...know things about them. But as you said before, I don't know what it is I know. I have knowledge but nowhere to go with it. I know they're mean and dangerous. Ruthless, even. I think they hurt my friend, Lenny. They use women. Abuse them. I'm not sure what else, but I know there's more. I know who they are, some of them anyway, what kinds of cars they drive, where they live, a little about how they operate."

I wipe the tear away with my fingers. No more fall. I became more sure of myself and less emotional as I laid it all out for him.

"I'd be careful. I'm going to get a gun and take self-defense classes and start working out. If nothing else, with the way they smoke, I'll be able to outrun them."

I see a ghost of a smile play across his features.

"I won't give up. Whether you let me help you or not. If you don't, I'll go ahead on my own. I have to see this through. I can't tell you why. I just have to do it."

I lift a hand and let it fall.

"You are quite something," he says softly.

I stare at him hoping he isn't going to try to sweet talk me out of my commitment with compliments and flattery. "I'm your daughter." Somehow, to me anyway, that says it all.

"Yes," he agrees. He stands and so do I. "It is late. You have given me much to consider."

"Does that mean you'll think about it?"

Again that ghost of a smile. "You have given me much to consider."

"That isn't an answer."

"No," he agrees.

I want to hug him and have him hug me back, but it doesn't feel quite right to attempt such a thing. Instead I stand on tiptoe and peck him on the cheek. "Bye, Dad." I tug a strand of his hair. "By the way, you need a haircut."

He squeezes my elbow before I slip out the door. "You will be careful, Tango."

"Yes."

The door clicks behind me.

Chapter Nine

Oh, that they would know what they are getting into!

I stick to the same pattern on the return trip to Wendy's, keeping to the landscaping, dodging behind strip plazas. I constantly swivel my head, trying to accustom my eyes to the play of dark and light, the shadows, to be alert for any movement. Every minute or so I look behind me. Although there's traffic along the highway, there are no pedestrians. I don't consider that unusual. Seagate is the kind of place where you need a car. The county finally implemented public transportation two years ago with bus routes. I've also noticed more and more taxis around town the past couple of years. But everyone I know has a car and no one I know walks anywhere if they don't have to. Plus, most of the businesses I pass are either closed or have shut down completely. The economy has not been kind to many of those living on the fringe of a wealthy community like Seagate. Only the strong survive.

The Wendy's is closed by the time I reach it, although there are lights on inside and I see a few workers upending chairs and mopping the floor. I skirt a round behind the building and stop short. My Jeep is not where I left it. I stare at the angled parking spaces, my gaze boring a hole into the one my Jeep had occupied. It's empty.

I have a sick, horrified, violated feeling in my gut. Somebody stole my car!

I do what any law-abiding citizen such as myself would do. I call the cops.

It is almost midnight. I think about calling someone to come get me. Who? Cody? Not without an explanation which I don't want to provide. Lenny? He lives so far out of town and he's still recovering from his accident. Joe? Joe has a real job and probably wouldn't appreciate a request to rescue me on the other side of town so late. Although he I knew he'd do it. My mother, Patrick, Sammi? No, no and no. My mother and Patrick would fuss and worry, ask why I'm in this part of town to begin with. Sammi has her own problems. I certainly can't contact my father, although I briefly think of returning to the motel. He'd probably give me a ride home, but paranoid as we both were about being seen together or followed, I decide that isn't a good idea either.

I spend twenty or so minutes cooling my heels sitting on the curb before a patrol unit from the sheriff's department arrives. I'd met the deputy,

Will Samson, once, months ago at Pelican Harry's when I was with Cody and Will remembers me. After he gives me a copy of the police report he offers me a ride home.

The cruiser drops me outside my apartment building entrance. I thank Will and trudge up the stairs. When I get to the second floor, Cody is leaning against the doorjamb, arms casually crossed over his chest, his apartment door open behind him. I stop at the top of the stairs and we stare at each other for a minute. This is becoming an all-too-familiar occurrence.

"Everything okay?" he asks.

"Somebody stole my Jeep," I tell him glumly.

He drops his casual stance and steps toward me. "What? Where? How?"

I've just been through all this with the deputy and I'll have to go through it with my insurance company tomorrow. I don't feel like explaining the situation to Cody because I know he'll ask more questions than I want to answer. "I left it parked outside a Wendy's for a little while. When I came back it was gone." I unlock my apartment door. He follows me inside.

I am drained and defeated. All I can think about is how things constantly go wrong for me lately. I have to open tomorrow and I have no way to get to work. Cody must have sensed that now was not the time for a barrage of questions. "Anything I can do?"

I hate to ask him, but I do. "Can you take me to work in the morning? I have to open."

He doesn't even groan at the idea of getting up at four-thirty a.m. He's still on paid leave. He can sleep all day tomorrow if he wants, and he probably would since apparently he's stopped sleeping at night. "I can do that. Do I get free coffee out of the deal?"

He chucks me under the chin and I work up a smile. "Of course."

"Aw, come here." He envelops me in one of his bear hugs and I decide I really, truly don't know what I'd do without him.

It is almost two o'clock the following afternoon when I walk out of Java Jake's and straight into Patrick. He gives me one of his delighted grins and opens his arms for a hug. "There's my girl. I didn't think you were here today. Where's your Jeep?"

"Are you going in? Can I get you coffee or something?"

"Yes, actually. I attended a seminar at the hospital and thought I'd stop before I go back to the office. I was hoping I'd run into you."

We go back inside and Patrick gets his coffee. "Want to sit outside for a minute?" he asks. "It's a beautiful day."

It is even though it's still pretty warm. The ceiling fans stir the air and in the shade it isn't too bad. I certainly don't want to spend any more time than I absolutely had to inside Java Jake's after being there for more than eight hours. Luckily, none of the Espresso Mafia are around at the moment.

"Jeep in the shop?" Patrick asks once we settle ourselves at a table in the no-smoking area.

"No. It was stolen last night."

"Stolen! From your apartment complex?"

"No. I left it parked at a Wendy's for a little bit while I...went to do something and when I got back it was gone."

I don't tell him which Wendy's and he doesn't ask. If he knew it was on the east side of town, he might pursue the question of what I was doing there in the first place. I doubt my mother has told Patrick that my father suddenly reappeared a few weeks ago. Even though we all love Patrick, he's an outsider. My mother, Sammi and I have been operating as our own unit for a long time.

"Your insurance will pay for a rental, surely? Until you replace it?"

"No. I was trying to save money so I dropped that coverage and raised my deductible." I hadn't been involved in a car accident in over five years and hadn't thought I'd need the extras on my insurance policy. Although a stolen car was always a possibility, I thought it was also highly unlikely.

"What will you do?"

I lift a hand and let it drop back to my lap. "I don't know. If the Jeep isn't recovered, the insurance will pay, less my deductible, of course, which should be just about enough to cover my car loan. Basically, I'm screwed. I don't have any savings and no money to put down on another car. I haven't figured it out yet. But I will."

Patrick regards me kindly with a little smile on his face. He leans forward. "I think I can help."

"No. I can't ask you to bail me out. This is my problem. I'll figure it out."

"But if you let me help, you will also solve a problem for me."

"How?"

He grins. "You know how much I love Monty," he begins.

I nod. Monty is Patrick's Lincoln Town Car that by my calculation has to be close to fifteen years old. Sammi and I dubbed it "The Hearse" not only because it was black, but because

Patrick keeps it polished to a high sheen at all times. Since he'd never had children, Monty is his baby. He's treated it lovingly since buying it new, as he often told us, when he reached gold level status with the life insurance company he represents.

"Of course, your mother, not so much." He fluttered a hand through the air as if my mother's opinion holds no sway with him. I know she's been on him since they got married to get rid of Monty and replace him with a newer model. Patrick has never shown any inclination to listen to her on this particular subject. Surely he doesn't plan to now. "I'd like to keep Monty, but I'd like to keep your mother, as well. I haven't told her this, but I've considered buying a new car. I know it would make her happy. She says only a fuddy-duddy would drive a car like Monty." Patrick looks offended at such an outlandish thought, but on this point I am certain my mother is on to something.

"I don't see what this has to do with me, though." I hope he isn't going to say what I think he's going to say.

"If I give Monty to you I know you'll take good care of him. I can keep him in the family, come visit him from time to time." What I want to say is, *Patrick, Monty's a car, for Pete's sake.* But I don't. Patrick is a sweet, sensitive, guy. He develops deep attachments to things as well as to people and once he does, he becomes quite protective of them. He's that way with my mother, with Sammi, and with me. I can't fault him for extending the same kind of loyalty to a car. I can't understand it either, but look at me. I'm not attached to anything or anyone. Still, do I really want to drive a fifteen-year-old Lincoln Town Car on a daily basis? No, I do not. Do I have a choice? Not unless I want to walk or get a bicycle.

"That's really generous of you, Patrick. I don't know what to say." I get a little choked up. My biological father certainly hasn't swept in to save the day. He probably doesn't know my Jeep is gone. How could he? Not like I could call him up and say, "Hey, Dad. I've got a problem. I need your help."

Why then, do I feel that by accepting Patrick's gift I am somehow turning my back on my father? I have no idea except I'm tired and I'm a jumble of conflicting emotions these days. My life has taken such odd turns in the past couple of months I almost feel like I can't keep track and I can't keep up.

"Tell you what, why don't you drive with me to the Cadillac dealership. I've taken a couple of test drives and I think I've got the sales manager right where I want him. You can drop me off and take Monty home. We'll deal with the paperwork later."

"Really, Patrick? You're sure?"

He stands and so do I. He leans down and kisses my cheek and pushes his fingers through my tangle of hair. "Because it's you, my girl, I'm sure."

That scares me a little. I'm not exactly what you'd call responsible. But I'll do my best to live up to Patrick's faith in me and take good care of Monty.

?

Chapter Ten

Your enemies shall bow low before you.

Joe calls when I get home that evening. He kind of knows my schedule, even though it varies from week to week. I must have told him I'd be off tomorrow night though because he wants to take me to dinner. But I've already accepted an invitation from Father Tom to visit Angel's Wings.

"I can't," I tell him. I'm bummed and I wonder if he can hear it in my voice. I hope so. "I have a prior engagement."

"Please tell me it's not with another guy," Joe groans.

I smile because I know this is part of him teasing me about Lenny and Cody who he considers his competition. Well, Lenny anyway.

"It is." I giggle because even though I'm not at all prone to giggling under normal circumstances, when I talk to Joe on the phone I tend to do it a lot.

"I should have known. I wish you had warned me that you were the most popular girl in Seagate when I first asked you out."

"I would have, but I wasn't. I'm not."

"Mmhmm. So who's my latest competition?"

"Father Tom."

"Father Tom? You're dating a priest?"

I laugh out loud. Joe sounds like he's only half joking. "I'm not dating him."

"Yet?"

"Joe. Be serious. Catholic priests aren't allowed to date."

"That doesn't stop some of them from what I've heard."

"I'm not dating Father Tom. He's a friend. I want to talk to him about something."

I wait while Joe digests this. "Are you cooking him dinner?"

"No, I'm going to the halfway house he runs. It's spaghetti night."

"Okay."

"Okay?" Does Joe think he's giving me permission?

"Spaghetti's not date food," he informs me with such authority that I don't argue. "So when can I see you?"

I look at my calendar where I've written my schedule. "I'm closing the next two nights." I wonder if he picks up on my disappointment.

"Bummer, but okay." We agree to dinner on my next night off. "I miss you," he says. I don't know about his cell phone radar, but mine picks up the sincerity in his voice.

"I miss you, too," I tell him softly.

I figure Father Tom is the one person I know that I can tell anything to, even that I swallow forbidden beans and temporarily turn into other entities, and my secrets will be safe with him. He won't judge me. He might not even think I'm crazy or making it all up. He might give me some guidance, because I feel very torn and confused.

The following evening I park Monty outside Angel's Wings. It's an unimpressive building in the low-rent area of Seagate. The place looks like it gets a fresh coat of paint on a regular basis which does little to hide the flaws in the façade. There are a couple of people hanging around in front smoking cigarettes. Someone tried to pretty the entrance up by placing a fountain with a statue of an angel on it, arms wide and welcoming. There isn't any water in the fountain, only some dried grime and a couple of cigarette butts.

I nod to the guys who watched me park and get out of my car. "I'm looking for Father Tom," I inform them.

One of the guys says, "He's in the kitchen. Go on in."

"Thanks."

The door opens into a wide homey space furnished with a faded sofa and well-worn chairs situated around a television. Beyond that is a dining area with mismatched chairs and a scarred wood table. I follow my nose to the kitchen and find Father Tom stirring sauce in a big pot. Another pot holds pasta in boiling water.

"Tee!" He puts down the spoon and gives me a quick hug. I give him the pound bag of Italian Roast I've brought from Java Jake's.

The kitchen is in the same kind of shape as the rest of the house. The appliances are old, the counter worn and stained, the linoleum peeling and scuffed. *Give me your tired and downtrodden.* That's what it makes me think of.

"Dinner's almost ready," Father Tom tells me.

I look around. There is a bowl of salad on the table and a loaf of bread. "Can I help?"

"You can get out plates and silverware." He points to a cabinet next to the sink and a drawer below it. "Let's see, there'll be eight of us."

"The spaghetti smells wonderful," I tell him. My stomach growls.

"It's one of the few meals I can make successfully." Father Tom and I have that in common. "We take turns with the chores here."

A few minutes later the residents join us. There is no bell or call to come and eat. Dinner is

served at six each evening. If you aren't
responsible enough to show up on time, you
don't eat, Father Tom explains. There are rules to
be abided by at Angel's Wings. Those who can't
handle the structured environment aren't
allowed to stay. I suppose that explains the small
number currently in residence.

Father Tom introduces me to the others, but
their names blur. They all seem pleasant enough,
although they are much like the place. Tired,
worn down. But they are survivors and they're
still hanging in there. I admire that.

Father leads us in grace and mostly it is a quiet
gathering with the occasional smatter of small
talk or Father asking the residents about their
days.

After we finish dinner I make a pot of coffee.
Father Tom leads me to his office. There is more
hand-me-down furniture in the form of a big
wood desk and mismatched bookshelves lining
two walls. There's enough room for what looks
like a reasonably comfortable chair which is
where Father Tom sits. There's a padded loveseat,
so I sit there. An end table with a lamp on it
occupies the adjacent corner.

All through dinner I tried to think how to
bring up what I want to know, but I don't know

how to start. I wonder now if I even should. What if there's some rule in the Catholic Church that if a priest discovers someone he thinks is seriously deranged he's obligated to contact the authorities? The police or the county mental health department or something?

If someone confesses to a murder, isn't it your moral duty to see that individual brought to justice? I try to remember every cop show I've ever seen that involved criminals confessing to priests. I decide before I tell him anything I should just ask Father Tom outright what his obligations are.

He seems only slightly surprised by my question. "Well, Tee, the thing is, someone might confess a crime to me during the sacrament of reconciliation, but I wouldn't necessarily know who it is. There's an element of privacy associated with confession between a priest and a confessor. Even when we're face-to-face, chances are good I wouldn't recognize the individual. Nor would I be able to ascertain if he's telling the truth. The best I could do, if he or she has committed a crime is urge the individual to go to the authorities and turn themselves in. I can offer them the solace of God's forgiveness if they're truly repentant, but forgiveness is a complicated thing. It isn't guaranteed just because you've shared whatever it is you've done with a priest and said you're sorry."

I take a sip of coffee and try to digest this bit of information. I also begin to question what exactly it is I want from Father Tom. I don't think it's forgiveness. Maybe it's validation that the course of action I'd decided on was the right one.

Father Tom wraps both his hands around his coffee mug and doesn't seem in any hurry for me to get to the point. From the moment I walked in the door he's act like he has all the time in the world. During dinner he told me he'd been on sabbatical for a couple of months and that's why I hadn't seen him until that night in the parking lot. He'd gone to Rome and then to a monastery in North Carolina where he fasted and prayed. He is the most serene, peaceful person I've ever met. Just being in the same room with him calms me.

"Father Tom, what if, let's say for example I killed someone, but I had a good reason for doing it."

He waits as if he expects me to continue. But when I don't say anything else, he says, "Like self-defense?"

I think about that for a moment. At no time had I been under direct attack by Randall Grimes. "More like to protect someone else. Or maybe a lot of other people."

Who knows how many more teenage girls Grimes might have gone after, raped and killed? Or how many cops he'd have taken down along the way.

Father Tom tilts his head. "One of the oldest philosophical questions in the world. One sacrifice for the greater good."

"That makes it sound almost noble."

"Here's the thing, Tee. Let's say you killed someone you considered to be evil. We're speaking in the hypothetical, of course." His blue eyes twinkle at me.

"Of course."

"You have proof of this individual's past evil deeds. Perhaps you even witnessed some of them."

I nod. "I did."

"Your fear is this individual will continue in his evil ways, that he will hurt others and you seek to prevent such an occurrence. You're certain your only option is to end his life."

"It was," I breathe.

"You feel justified in what you did. You don't regret it." This comes out as a statement but there is a question behind it.

I squirm and set my mug on the end table. "I want to know I did the right thing. At the time I didn't think I had a choice. I didn't think about it very long. I couldn't. I had to act." I take myself back to that jail cell and I know without a doubt that if I had to do it again I would. I'd been certain then I was doing the right thing. I'd felt compelled to do it. I wasn't sure why I was second-guessing myself now.

"Ah, well, I can't tell you if you did the right thing or not. My sense is you have no regret, you simply want to justify your actions. Without going into more detail, which frankly, Tee, I'd rather you didn't—it's much easier for both of us if we consider this discussion in the abstract—I can tell you this: My belief is that God is always waiting for His children to turn to him. Human beings do evil, have done evil since the beginning, since God kicked Adam and Eve out of the garden for disobeying him. But evil is not a life sentence. Human beings can and do turn from their evil ways. Can a murderer be forgiven? The answer is yes. If he is truly repentant. Can killing another human being ever be justified? I believe the answer to that is yes as well. The key, Tee, is what's in your heart. That's what God looks at. What's in your heart and what you choose to do in the future. That's why, at the end of every confession a priest says, 'Go and sin no more.'

I try to absorb everything Father Tom has told me and for an unreligious person like me, it isn't easy.

"Father Tom—"

"You know, Tee, you can call me 'Tom' if you want. I don't expect my friends to use my title."

"Oh, okay." Admittedly, I glow a little knowing I've been elevated to the status of one of Father Tom's—er—*Tom's* friends. Like I've been given admission to a small inner circle. "One more question." I think for a moment about how to ask. "If you felt you had to do something to stop something bad from happening, but in the process, people you loved might get hurt because of your actions, should you go ahead and do it anyway?"

"Yes."

I stare at Tom. I didn't expect such a simple answer. "Yes? That's it?"

Tom chuckles. "You want a long drawn-out philosophical answer based on theology?"

I laugh. "I think that's what I expected."

"Tee, you have a lot of questions about good and evil and their places in the world. I don't know if this will help you, but Jesus, who did nothing but good during his time on earth, had followers who suffered greatly for following in his footsteps. They were imprisoned, tortured, killed.

It still happens today. Good people suffer. Evil is often allowed to flourish. That's the way of our fallen world.

"You, Tee, cannot prevent it, as much as you might like to. No one can. If you have righteousness on your side, if in your heart you believe you are being led to fight evil, those closest to you may suffer. But the reason they suffer is because of evil, not because of the good you are trying to do.

"Is this helping you at all?" he asks gently.

"I think so. It's giving me a lot to think about."

Chapter Eleven

How could one single enemy chase a thousand of them,

I arrive early for my appointment and have to sit in Dr. Parker's waiting area. Her office is only one room, but the waiting area is just at the end of the hallway and she'll come get her patients after the previous session ends.

The furniture here is rattan with flowered cushions on a maroon background. It isn't all that comfortable or attractive, but usually I don't have to spend much time sitting on the loveseat next to the glass-topped table. There are a few magazines stacked on it, but nothing that interests me. Mostly they are Florida lifestyle magazines and I already know enough about the Florida lifestyle.

I hear her door close at the end of the hall and she bids her patient good-bye. He or she heads in the opposite direction toward the stairs or the elevator. Dr. Parker has her office set up so the patients don't have to encounter each other on the way in or out. Imagine if they were passing acquaintances or coworkers. I wonder briefly if any of them are Java Jake's regulars. I wouldn't be surprised. In a lot of ways, Seagate is a small town.

"Hello, Tee. How are you?" Dr. P. smiles at me and her greeting holds its usual warmth.

I stand. "I'm okay."

"Let's get started then, shall we?"

I follow her to her office and settle in my usual place. I haven't been here since my very first transformative episode when I turned into a fly and prevented a date rape. The second time I'd been in the body of a butterfly. I had been so freaked out by those episodes. I hadn't understood what was happening to me and neither had Dr. P. She tried to help me with what she thought was disassociation. When I figured out the beans were responsible, I cancelled the follow-up appointment. I can't tell Dr. P. or anyone else for that matter what causes my "episodes." I'm not here to talk about myself in any case. I want to know about Sammi.

"You haven't been here for several weeks, Tee. How have things been going for you?"

Briefly I think about how much fun it would be to yank Dr. P.'s chain. I can tell her about my time in the body of a frog and what I witnessed. I can tell her how I almost turned into a frog for real. Except she'd probably think I am certifiably crazy. I might risk being sent to the county mental health facility. She could have me Baker-acted and stick me in there for three days. In such a place I'll have no access to my beans. I'll turn into whatever I was last. A lizard. No thank you.

"Things are going okay for me," I reply. "But I'm concerned about my sister."

If this disconcerted her she doesn't show it. "Your sister."

"Yes. Her name's Sammi. I don't know if you remember her from our family sessions a few years ago—"

"I remember her."

"I'm worried about her."

Dr. P. inclines her head and stares at me intently. "Why is that?"

"I think she's engaging in self-destructive behavior."

"What kind of self-destructive behavior?"

"Cutting herself for one thing."

"Did Sammi tell you this? Have you seen evidence of it?"

"Sammi didn't tell me. I'm sure she doesn't want anyone to know."

"Are you certain—"

"Yes. Look, it doesn't matter how I know about it. What matters is she's my sister and I love her and I want to help her. There's more."

"Go on."

"She's seeing someone."

"That's not unusual, is it? If I recall, your sister is quite attractive. I'm sure men are interested in her."

"True. She's never had a problem finding boyfriends, but this is different."

"Different how?"

"She's not seeing a man."

"Oh?"

"She's seeing a woman."

"Ah."

"She's seeing you, Dr. Parker. But not as a patient."

Dr. P.'s eyes widen and her lips compress, but other than that she doesn't show any surprise or embarrassment. "You didn't find out about this from Sammi," she says.

"No."

"What is it you want, Tee?"

"I want to help Sammi."

"Well, then." She smiles sadly. "You and I want the same thing."

She says that and waits. I guess it's my turn to speak, but I don't know exactly what to say.

I'm now even sure why I was so compelled to come here and confront Dr. P. Sammi's relationship with her is none of my business. Except it sort of is. Dr. P. is *my* doctor. Sammi is *my* sister.

"I think she's sad," I say. "Confused. I don't like that she hurts herself."

"Tee, I can't discuss Sammi with you without her permission. I can't discuss my relationship with her with you. It wouldn't be appropriate. We can talk about your relationship with her if you like, or we can talk in generalities about individuals with psychological histories similar to your sister's. Anything else is out of the question."

That's about what I expected Dr. P. to say. I have no idea why but I feel much better now that she knows that I know. "How can I help her?" is what I ask because when you get down to it, it's what I really want to know.

I leave Dr. P.'s office with a folder stuffed full of handouts on cutting and a reading list of books where I can find more in-depth information. I can't help but wonder how much our family history has to do with Sammi's behavior now. If she knew the truth about our father, for example, would it help her?

I call Sammi on the way to my car. As usual I get her voice mail. I leave her a message anyway, that I am thinking about her and thought maybe she'd like to get an early lunch and that I'd call her later.

When I get to work that afternoon, I put the empty prescription bottle I brought from home into the pocket of my apron. Never again will I be caught without easy access to a forbidden bean. I have run numerous scenarios through my head. What if I go on vacation? What if I'm in an accident and hospitalized. What if what if what if? What if I get fired from Java Jake's? Or transferred to another store? Does every store have a bag of those forbidden beans hidden somewhere on the premises? Were there others like me who have discovered their magical power? I don't know. I have no way of knowing. I'm not sure I want to know. What I do know is that I'm not going to risk the consequences of not consuming a bean at least once every seven days.

Jerry's shift ends shortly after mine begins. "Good job on the count," he says.

"Thank you." Jerry always sticks me with the weekly inventory count. It is a pain in the ass and I don't enjoy it. He's never complimented me on it before.

I find a chance to scoot into the storeroom on my second ten-minute break. I don't waste any time uncovering and dislodging my bag of beans from its hiding place. I push the bottle I brought down into the bag and fill it with beans. I can't help but stare at the beans surrounded by amber-colored plastic before I put the cap back on the bottle. They glisten and wink up at me. Once again I feel that pull toward them. Sick. I am an addict. That's all there is to it. I can't give up my beans. I have to have one at least every seven days or I'll go through what I am very afraid will be an unending withdrawal experience. Worse than a heroin addict, even. The difference being if I'd chosen heroin, I'd have known about its addictive properties.

I'd been warned, though, hadn't I? I drop the vial into my apron pocket and stare at the warning printed on the bag. DO NO OPEN. DO NOT USE. I'd ignored it, just as I supposed anyone did with warnings about using cocaine or heroin or crystal meth. Or cigarettes. Knowing bad things will happen isn't enough to stop us from experimenting. I can't even justify my curiosity. I'd been warned. I'd ignored the warning. Simple as that.

I'd been warned about the Albanians, too, just as my father had. We'd both ignored those warnings as well.

I don't have a choice. Today is day seven. I have to swallow a bean. I choose one and take a few moments to let it lay in the palm of my hand while I stare at it mesmerized. How can something so small be so powerful? I hold it between my thumb and forefinger for a second before placing it on my tongue. Once again the coating melts away quickly, frustrating me that there is so little of it, that I can't compare it to anything I've ever tasted. Reluctantly I swallow the bean. I stare down into the bag once again before slowly rolling the silver foil down and pushing the bag back into hiding.

I arrange the syrup bottles back on the shelf and stand, dusting myself off before I open the door.

Like any addict I do what I have to do to survive.

Chapter Twelve

And deadly serpents Crawling in the dust

I raise my head to survey my surroundings. Directly in front of me, several hundred feet away, is a gray stucco building. It looks like a house, but there are two oversized garage doors on one side of it. There is a concrete pad along the back and all the windows are covered with metal hurricane shutters.

I am on the damp ground, surrounded by scrub brush about two feet high. Darkness is creeping in, so I figure it must be eight-thirty or nine. I take a peek over my shoulder only to discover I have no shoulders. Nor do I have to worry about what to call my hands, feet or legs because I don't have those either. What I do have is a long, narrow, shiny black body, which grows narrower the closer it gets to the end.

I drop my head to the ground and if I had hands I'd cover my eyes with them. It's hard to describe how disconcerting it is to be operating as a human and then to suddenly find myself in the body of something else. In this case evidently I'm a black racer. They're pretty common in south Florida. They aren't venomous and they can move pretty fast. Finally, at least I am inside a fast-moving body which should cut down on my clumsiness. Although come to think of it, during my time as a gecko I'd skittered around pretty quickly, too.

The last thing I remember is being at the desk in the back counting Bryce's till before we closed up for the night at Java Jake's. I know from past experience the auto-pilot part of me that was left behind in my body could handle the routine closing tasks like counting the safe and setting the alarm. I'm not worried. About that anyway.

I lift my head a little. Might as well go investigate the house. The storm shutters make it appear unoccupied, but at the same time, the place doesn't look exactly deserted. I slither experimentally, moving silently through the scrubby weeds. Easy peasy. And subtle. I could get used to this. Too bad I can't be a snake all the time. Spying on the Espresso Mafia would be easy. Then again, after my experience of nearly returning to a frog-like state, the last thing I want is to be a snake full-time.

I undulate my way forward, pausing about fifty feet from the concrete pad, tilting my head to listen. I think I hear a vehicle approaching. I slither parallel to the pad until I'm past the house and raise my head. Sure enough, a panel delivery van has reached the end of a turnaround in the concrete drive. The driver executes a three-point turn and backs the van up to the garage door. Odd. His headlights are off. He kills the engine and climbs out.

One of the overhead doors rumbles up, but no light spill out from inside. I slither closer, to the edge of the driveway. I am black and without light, no one is going to notice me. I need to be higher because my night vision isn't so good. I can see shoes and pants and that's about it. There aren't any nearby trees or bushes I can climb. If I can even climb which is questionable. Surely I could twine myself around the trunk of a bush and work my way up through the branches, given the opportunity.

I try to see inside the garage, but all I see is gloomy darkness. The driver and whoever put the garage door up exchange a few words in a foreign language. You'd think I'd have heard enough Albanian-speak by now to recognize it when I hear it, but I don't. My only defense is that usually I hear the words in accented English. This had that same Eastern European rhythm to it, but how can I know it isn't Romanian, or Czech or any other language spoken in that region? Bulgarian. I need to be objective.

The driver opens the double back doors of the van. I hear a sliding sound as they reach in. With one on either side, they lift something, a wooden crate perhaps, out of the van and carry it into the garage by the dim interior light of the van. No other lights. No stars. No moon. How can they even see where they're going? I can barely see the vague outlines of them now. Mostly I sense their motion and I can hear what they're doing. Their night vision must be better than mine. Footsteps recede into the garage and repeat, and it sound like crates are being slid on top of each other. I count eight trips. I want to get closer, even if it means getting trapped in the garage.

A lighter clicks and in the brief flare of the flame I see the face of the individual with the cigarette. I recognize him!

Whoa! What's that? Something slithers up close to me and if I could scream I would. Instead my scream comes out as a sort of semi-silent hissing sound. Instinctively I turn to look at whatever just rubbed up against me, but I can't see a thing.

Yikes! Hey! Stop that! I hiss again and slither away as fast as I can. Whoever, whatever is after me doesn't give up easily. He—how do I know it's a he?—is practically on top of me. His body feels bigger and heavier than mine, and—oh, wait, *that's* how I know it's a he.

Defense? What defense do I have in my present state against one of the opposite sex of my own species who apparently is in a romantic mood? *Get off me*!

I hiss and slither trying to escape his amorous overtures but he is having none of it. *Snake rape! Help me*! He probably thinks I'm playing hard to get. I think of that girl Lindsey I'd saved from being date-raped by that moron Tyler during my episode as a biting fly. She'd had hands and fingernails and her whole human body to fight back with and still, if not for my intervention, she hadn't stood a chance against Tyler's superior strength and determination. At the moment I have none of my human attributes or limbs. Other than most of my thinking, pissed-off self, that is.

I slither blindly through the weed-choked lot with no idea where I'm going. I can't see anything and have to rely purely on instinct. Never have I wished for my legs, feet and hands quite so much. Oh, if only I could zap back into my human body right now before Mr. Macho has his way with me.

All of a sudden I stop moving. My slithering ability leaves as quickly as it arrived and I am face down in dirt and weeds. My admirer slithers against me once more, giving me the heebie geebies, until he realizes there is no longer any point in pursuing me and slips away through the grass. I shove myself up to stand on shaky legs and brush myself off. I am still covered in black, but I'm in my Java Jake's work clothes sans the tan apron.

I shiver even though it's probably eighty degrees and ninety-five percent humidity. Did I somehow summon my body to me? Can my thoughts control the power of the beans? My legs go out from under me and I collapse in a heap right there on the ground.

Always before my human body was ...where it was. Most of me left it and went into whatever I temporarily turned into. When the effect of the bean wore off the part of me that had left went back into my human body and I was whole again. My body never came to me. Until now. How...where...why do I have that power? *Do* I have that power? Or is this some new aspect of bean consumption? Perhaps the symptoms of my addiction will morph and change the longer I continue to consume the beans.

I cover my mouth with my hands to hold in the low moan that threatens to escape. I'll never be me again. Just me. The way I used to be. If I don't consume a bean on a regular basis, I'll turn back into a human form of whatever was last. I'll continue to zap into other bodies temporarily before returning to my own original one. Or my human body will return itself to me.

Beam me up, Scotty. I always thought the ability to transform oneself from one place to another was a pretty cool idea. No long airline flight, no road trip. Just stand on that circle in the transporter room and let Scotty do his thing. Zap, you're on the planet. Zap, you're back on the ship. But that was *fiction*! A TV show. A movie. It wasn't real life.

How about *Bewitched*? I'd watched those reruns of the original television show as a kid and I'd loved the idea that all Samantha had to do was twitch her nose and she could make magic happen. Things appeared or disappeared under her spell, often with hilarious or detrimental results. Is that what will happen to me? What if I'm at work or on a date or *driving* for God's sake and my body just leaves? What will happen then? I can see the opening line of the article beneath the headline in the *Seagate Sentinel*, "A 1992 Lincoln Town Car, apparently driving itself, crashed into the..."

Just when I think I've learned how to control the power of the beans, they throw me a curve ball. Dampness from the ground below me begins to seep uncomfortably into the seat of my pants. I try standing again to discover I'm a little more stable this time.

I still have no idea where I am. I do a hundred and eighty-degree turn to get my bearings. I'd been slithering away from the house so it must be behind me somewhere. I pause and listen. There are a few night noises: rustling in the weeds; a cricket sings nearby and then abruptly stops. Perhaps my would-be boyfriend stopped for a snack.

I am a little creeped out by how incredibly dark it is. I must be fairly far out of town, somewhere out in the undeveloped wilds of Silvergate, no doubt. There has to be a road, however, or that van wouldn't have had access to the house. I take a couple of tentative steps in the direction I decide the house must be. My hands brush against my pants pockets and I realize I'm not as helpless as I thought. From one pocket I withdraw my cell phone. From the other, my car keys. Woo-hoo! Jackpot!

My cell phone has juice and surprisingly, it also has reception. I have the tiny flashlight on my key ring, the same one that had helped Joe and me find Scorch out in the woods. My cell phone won't be much use unless I can tell someone where I am, so I pocket it.

I squeeze the flashlight and the pinpoint of light it provides gives me some comfort. I sweep the light in an arc in front of me and think can just make out the outline of the house. I turn the light off just in case there is anyone still around and start forward in the dark.

I try to be quiet. Luckily the ground is damp and I have on my thick-soled work shoes. I wonder if the guy who was inside the garage lives here.

When I stumble onto the concrete pad I stand still and wait. For what I don't know. I have visions of blinding lights coming on all at once spotlighting me as an intruder, like in those prison movies when someone tries to break out. For all I know this place has motion detectors I can trip in the dark that will aim flood lights at me as if I were a star on the red carpet at a movie premiere.

Why do I think the place might have an alarm system of some sort to detect intruders such as myself? Because the van approached with its headlights turned off? Because they unloaded the van under cover of complete darkness? Clearly *they*, whoever *they* are, do not want to be detected.

I have a debate with myself while minutes tick by. I hear a far distant rumble of thunder, too far away to mean a storm close by. I risk turning on my tiny light once more and sweep it across the back of the house. The van is gone. It must have left while I was trying to escape the other snake. I'd been so focused on getting away from him, I wasn't able to watch what was happening here.

I cross the driveway, quickly flashing the light to find that both the garage doors are closed. Circling around to the front of the house I see the same hurricane shutters covering the windows and a solid front door painted the same unrelenting gray as the house. The far side proves no more interesting with only two more shuttered windows.

No alarms or lights come on. I don't notice the whir of security cameras following my movements, although I suppose it is possible this place possesses security equipment that I wouldn't be able to see. Infrared cameras, maybe that detect all motion. My imagination ran wild, but since nothing happened, I step over to one of the windows and test the shutter. It doesn't budge when I push on it. I circle the house, trying each of the shutters and then the front door, which is locked.

The set-up makes me think of an abandoned building project, which is not all that uncommon in and around Seagate. Builders often run out of money mid-way through construction and walk away leaving everything as is. Especially with the economic downturns of the past couple of years where it seems real estate development came to standstill, partially completed houses like this one are common.

I can't get inside to see what's in those crates. I flash my light a bit as I cross back to the driveway. About ten feet from the house the concrete ends and become a gravel drive. I turn my light off figuring as long as I can hear the crunch of gravel under my feet, I won't have a problem following it and I'm right. Until I walk face first into what turns out to be a chain link fence. I rub my nose and flash my light to discover a fence all along the front of the property. I estimate it to be about eight feet high with those little pointy ends along the top. The gate over the drive is on wheels so it will roll back to let a vehicle through. It is also chained and padlocked, so I can't get out that way. It looks like up and over for me, an idea I approach with trepidation.

In the movies cops and criminals seem to have absolutely no problem scaling chain link fences, clambering up and dropping neatly on the other side. I sincerely doubt it's as easy as they make it look. I shove my keys in my pocket and take hold of the metal as high as I can, find a toehold and start up. Probably I can climb up easily enough, it's the going over part I'm not too crazy about, especially with those spiky bits of wire at the very top.

I need to work on my upper body strength, because by the time I get to the top, my arms are shaking. My fingers are sore from gripping the thin metal and I have serious doubts about how to get myself over the top without ripping my clothes to shreds and gouging myself.

I do the best I can, balancing myself with a hand on either side of the crossbar and walking my feet up and over. I'm about to congratulate myself on my success when I lose my hold on both the bar and the wire and drop six feet to land hard on my keister in the gravel.

I sit there for a moment realizing I'd have been smarter to climb over on either side of the driveway because then at least I'd have landed in the cushion of dirt and weeds. I'm injured beyond repair, so I get to my feet and rub my posterior while I get my bearings.

There is an unpaved road running in front of the house. I can just make out what looks like a streetlight in the distance. All I can sense and see in the other direction is darkness, which probably leads to a dead end. There's probably a canal running perpendicular to the road. That's how most of the outlying areas of Silvergate are set up. Residential streets lead off both sides of the main thoroughfares straight into dead ends and canals.

I flash my light briefly and it's enough to confirm the dead end twenty feet from where I stand. If I work my way through the brush, I know I'll find a canal.

I set off toward the light. My tired mind turns over my recent out-of-body experience as I limp along flashing my light every once in awhile. The road is deserted and even though there may be other residences along the way they are as dark as everything else or possibly set so far back from the road that I can't see them. I don't notice any mailboxes or driveways along the way, but that doesn't mean much. I could have easily missed them.

When that cigarette lighter flared earlier I'd fixed on the face of the man who'd lit it. It was the same guy who'd shown up at my door with a fake flower delivery last month. Stupid, I know to open the door and let him in, but for a girl who doesn't get flowers very often, it didn't occur to me that it was a set-up until it was too late.

He was one of the Albanians, sent to do their dirty work, after I'd snooped around a little too much in their business. He'd warned me first with his fists and the toe of his boot and then with his menacing words laden with some truly disgusting halitosis an inch from my face. That's when I grabbed his balls and squeezed at the same moment Magic dug his claws into the guy's back. Between the two of us we'd sent him on his way.

I hadn't seen him before or since until tonight so I have to assume he is one of their gophers used for the intimidation work as well as the heavy lifting. It takes me less than fifteen minutes to reach the cross road. I look up at the street sign visible in the light from the streetlamp. Sixty-second Avenue Southwest. Oh, yeah. I am way out in the boonies, almost at the county line. The cross street is Everglades Boulevard which, after ten or fifteen miles would get me back into Seagate. I cross to the right side of the street and start walking.

I think about calling Lenny. He'd be the most likely to answer and the most likely to come to my aid with the least number of questions and the least amount of suspicion. Still, after his supposed accident, I don't want to involve him unless I absolutely have to. I'm on my own. Alone again. Naturally.

That far off storm wasn't as far off as I thought because it started to rain. Lightly at first but then it turns into a pretty good steady downpour. That's not unusual this time of year and it probably won't last long. Just long enough to soak me good and make walking even less enjoyable than it already is. Everglades Boulevard is a two-lane blacktop punctuated with streetlights at all the crossroads which are about every half mile or so, I guess. I walk along the edge of the pavement so I can step off onto the shoulder if a car approaches from behind.

According to my phone it's after midnight. I don't expect much traffic to pass me at this hour.

I pass Sixtieth Avenue and then Fifty-eighth before headlights shine behind me. I step off to the shoulder assuming the car will go on by. It doesn't occur to me to try to flag it down. Who knows what might happen if I get into a car with a stranger? Even if I am soaking wet and close to exhaustion, I won't hitchhike and certainly not in this neighborhood.

The car flies past me but suddenly brakes and backs up. I stop, ready to run if I need to, though where I will run to, I have no idea. I don't fancy crossing the muddy swale I know runs along the side of the road a few feet away.

The car is a silver Honda Accord that looks to be a few years old. When it draws even with me, the passenger window lowers and a woman dressed in maroon surgical scrubs leans across the seat. "You need a ride, hon?"

She is about fifty, with a head of over-processed golden blond frizz and a face freckled more from sun than nature. She looks harmless enough. When I don't respond immediately, she flips the lock from the inside. "Get in if you're comin.' I got to get to the hospital."

I open the door and get in and she takes off, her tires spinning a bit before they find traction on the wet pavement. She glances my way. "Man troubles?"

"What makes you say that?"

She lifts a shoulder and lets it fall. "You're out walkin' in the middle of the night. Ain't got no purse or nothin.' Figure some man done kicked you out of the house or you decided to run without plannin' too far ahead. Plus you're limping. He beat you?"

"No. I fell."

She snorts. "Oldest line in the book."

She shoves the car's lighter in and rummages in the center console for a cigarette. In spite of the rain, she lowers the window on her side about an inch. After she lights up and blows out a stream of smoke in the direction of the window she glances my way for a second. "Name's Darlene."

"Tee."

"That it? Just Tee?"

"Yes. Are you a nurse?"

"Surgical tech. My night to take call. I can drop you anywhere between here and the hospital. Or you can wait at the hospital and stay at my place for a day or two."

"You don't know me. That's pretty generous of you."

She glances at me again. "Wouldn't be the first time I've made the offer."

"Thanks, Darlene. But I've got a place to go. You can drop me at the corner of Vanderbilt and Airport Road. It's not too far from there."

"All right."

We stop talking after that. Darlene turns up the radio a bit and we listen to country singers wail about their lot in life while the wipers slap across the windshield. When she stop to let me out, she hand me a business card. "You take care now, Tee."

"I will. Thanks for the ride." The rain has let up to a sprinkle and I look at the card. *Shelter for Victims of Abuse, Colfax County, Florida.* A phone number is included but no address.

I drag my tired, aching self the mile or so to my apartment. Monty is parked in the lot right where he should be. I let myself in to my apartment noting that my purse and the bag I carry to and from work to hold my apron, snacks and other miscellaneous items is on the table where I normally drop them when I get home. Everything made it back to the apartment except me.

I close the door behind me and a hand clamps over my mouth. Before I can get a scream going for the hand to muffle I hear a low male voice. "Tango."

What comes out of my mouth is an incomprehensible version of the word, "Daddy."

He takes his hand away and we stare at each other in the dim light illuminating the room from the half-closed blinds. "I did not mean to startle you."

That quick pump of adrenaline had shot through me so fast, it left me sagging.

"For someone who never means to startle me, you sure do it a lot."

"I apologize."

I am incredibly uncomfortable. I want a shower and I want my bed almost more than I want to have a conversation with my father. At the moment I don't have the mental resources to spar with him. "This really isn't a good time," I inform him.

I bend to untie my shoes, toeing them off and then peeling off my damp socks.

"Are you all right?" he asks.

"Just peachy," I quip. I incline my head toward the door. "Do you mind? I'd really like to shower and get ready for bed."

When did I turn into such a bitch? I've wanted a reunion with my father since early childhood. I've seen him a handful of times and now I'm kicking him out of my apartment. What is wrong with me?

If I surprised him or hurt his feelings, it doesn't show in his expression. "Of course." He nods in that curt way of his. "I will visit at a more convenient time."

He waits a moment, perhaps hoping I'll change my mind. When I don't say anything, he says, "Take care, Tango," and leaves.

I drag off my wet clothes and leave them in the laundry room before I get in the shower and let warm water pound me. My left buttock hurts. I bet I'll have on colossal bruise there by morning.

This is the first time I've been left hanging so to speak when I transform back into human form. The first few times, back when I was zapped into the bodies of various insects, it happened at night, often when I was asleep. A couple of times

I was at work or coming home from work and all of a sudden POW! I'd be back in my body, steaming milk or walking up the steps to my apartment.

My human body never reunited with me at the scene. This was a first and something I definitely couldn't control. Imagine if I'd turned back into myself while I was a wasp or a dragonfly, buzzing around one minute and falling to the ground the next. I'd just basically materialize out of nowhere as far as any human observers would know. I could end up on the road and get hit by a car. Or land on somebody's windshield.

I guess I was lucky this time. I was already on the ground, but still it was disconcerting and disorienting to realize this could happen and I couldn't control it.

After my shower I swallow a couple of ibuprofen hoping they will ease my discomfort. I'm hungry but too tired to eat.

I didn't even asked my father why he'd come or how he got in to my apartment. Or when I'd see him again. I almost don't care. Vaguely I wonder if all of our future encounters are going to begin with him clamping his hand over my mouth or holding a gun to my head.

I can't think any more.

I crawl into bed and pass out.

Chapter Thirteen

Fight for him against his enemies

I swim up from sleep to an insistent knocking on my door. After squinting at the alarm clock and determining it is barely nine, I drop my head back on the pillow with a groan. I am so not ready to get up. The knocking continues which means whoever is out there—it's probably Cody— isn't going to give up,

I drag my robe on and shuffle to the door. Magic streaks across the living room and darts behind the couch. I peek through the peephole and see Cody. "You can stop knocking now," I call irritably through the door before I undo the locks and open it. He doesn't stop knocking, of course, until I have the door all the way open. Then he grins and holds up a bag from the bagel store before he strides past me to the kitchen.

"I didn't get coffee because I know you won't drink anything but Java Jake's, so you'll have to make some."

I yawn and follow him into the kitchen. I would so rather be in bed, but my stomach growls reminding me I didn't have anything to eat last night. I am off today anyway, so if I decide to nap later there is nothing to stop me. I go through my coffee-making ritual while Cody puts bagels on plates, slices them and pops them into the toaster oven. My brain has yet to kick into gear. I lean against the counter listening to the sputter of the coffee maker and watch while Cody opens a tub of cream cheese and gets two butter knives out of a drawer. I yawn again. I am going to need a lot of coffee this morning.

"To what do I owe the pleasure of this early morning bagel delivery?"

"Early morning? I waited until after nine. What's with you? I thought you'd be up by now."

"Late night," I mutter as I turn to get mugs for the coffee.

"Hot date?" Cody teases.

I can't control my shudder of revulsion at the memory of my near snake rape incident. "I wish."

"So what'd you do? Close?"

"Uh-huh." As far as I know.

"Hey, what's this?"

Cody spied the card Darlene had given me. I'd left it on the counter when I'd stripped off my clothes last night. "What do you need with the abused women's shelter? Did Joe—?"

"Of course not," I scoff. "Don't be ridiculous."

Cody crosses his arms over his chest and scowls at me. "He better not."

I roll my eyes. "Someone just gave me the card, okay. I didn't ask for it and I don't need it." I take the card and toss it in the junk drawer. The coffeemaker gives its final sputter at the same time the toaster oven dings. I pour coffee while Cody deals with the bagels. We go around to sit on the stools on the other side of the counter.

"You working today?" he asks after a few sips of coffee and a couple of bites of bagel.

"I'm off."

"What are you going to do?"

"I'm going gun-shopping." *And you're not going to talk me out of it.*

"Tee—"

"What?" I say hotly. "It's my right as an American citizen to own a gun. What is your problem?"

Cody shakes his head and addresses his bagel. "I think it's a bad idea. I don't know why you think you need one."

"You have one," I grumble.

"I'm a cop."

"Yeah, but you have a gun of your own, too. Not just the one they issued you when you became a deputy."

"Everybody needs a back-up."

"I'm getting a gun. End of discussion. Do you want to go with me?" It hadn't occurred to me to invite Cody before since he was so against the idea to begin with but I realize now I'd appreciate his presence and expertise.

"If you're hell-bent on getting a gun, I'll go with you. I got nothing better to do."

"You will?" My delight must have shown on my face. He ducks his head. I reached over and give him a half hug. "Thanks."

We finish our bagels and coffee and Cody goes back to his place to change clothes while I get dressed. After the discussions I've had with my car insurance company, we calculated that the replacement value of the Jeep was just about what I owed on the loan. Since I now had no car payment, I'd have extra money every month. Extra money to spend on things like a gun, self-defense classes and a new computer.

In spite of his misgivings, Cody is surprisingly helpful, steering me to the best gunshop in town, where, because he accidentally on purpose lets it slip that he is a deputy, the owner gives me a nice discount. There is a bunch of paperwork and a three-day waiting period after I buy my compact Ruger before I can pick it up. It's perfect for concealed carry. Included with my purchase were three free lessons at the adjoining gun range. I take advantage of the first one with Cody there to coach me along with the instructor.

I've never held a gun before. The closest I've been to a gun is seeing the butt of Cody's service revolver when he's in uniform. Or more recently, when my father held that gun to my head.

I feel a new sense of power holding my gun in my hand and firing it at a paper target. It takes me a few times before I hit the outline of a human body in a way that will do any significant damage. The instructor, Bill, is an old retired cop, seventy if he's a day, but he knows his stuff. He is firm in his instructions, offering helpful hints on how to improve my aim, advising me to relax my shoulders and hold the gun with both hands to steady it until I get used to the feel of it.

The Ruger model I chose is deceptively lightweight and has minimum recoil. I love it.

By the time the lesson is over, I've hit my target close enough to the heart to do some serious damage several times. Both Cody and Bill strongly suggest I aim for a shoulder if possible, because, they intimate, I won't want to know what it feels like to kill my target.

I don't bother to inform them that I already know what it feels like to kill someone who richly deserves to die. I didn't use a gun, but I'd killed Randall Grimes before he could be set free to rape and murder another young girl. I don't regret it. I did what had to be done. Owning a gun won't change that. I have no intention of using it to kill anyone unless I absolutely have to. But I won't think twice about using it for self-defense, even if all I do is cause enough bodily injury to slow down an attacker so I can get away.

One of Cody's conditions of gun shopping with me is that I enroll in the Sheriff Department's four-hour gun safety class and I agree. I want to know everything there is to know about how to safely own and handle a gun.

Chapter Fourteen

He will watch their power ebb away

I wander through the Promenade Mall for twenty minutes waiting for my father to show up. I look at window displays for clothes and shoes and jewelry. I'm starting to wonder why I bothered to show up here.

Because he asked me to. Actually, he didn't ask. He texted my cell from a number I didn't recognize. *Meet me at Promenade Mall Saturday at one.*

To which I texted back, *Who is this?*

He didn't reply.

I got off work early and like a fool I made the thirty minute drive to the mall, which is in the next county, I might add. He didn't say where to meet him, so I parked and came inside and now I'm meandering. It's a big mall. He could be anywhere. Or not. I don't know why I was so certain the message was from my father.

I pull out my phone and check the time again. One twenty-three. Great. Not only did I waste a whole lot of gas due to Monty's gas-guzzling engine, I'd come here for nothing. I should know better. My father hadn't been there my whole life. Why did I think he'd show up now? He set me up. What if someone else sent that text? A lump of disappointment settles in my throat.

I'll walk to the end of this section of the mall, I decide, turn around at the entrance to Dillard's and head for home. Maybe, just so the trip isn't entirely wasted, I'll treat myself to a chimichanga and a Corona Light at Iguana Mia. It is right next to the mall and I hardly ever get to eat there.

I do a one-eighty in front of Dillard's, put some purpose in my stride and think of the big basket of homemade chips and salsa they'll set before me while I wait for my food. My mouth waters just thinking about.

"Just keep walking," he says, as he falls into step beside me.

My heart does a little giddy-up but I pretend I don't know he's there.

"We'll go to your car," he informs me after a bit. First we have to dodge a mother pushing a double stroller with several toddlers hanging onto it and then a gaggle of teenage girls giggling and texting. Behind them is a group of teenage boys shuffling along and pretending they have no interest in the girls.

Pumpkin spice and candy apple scents waft out of the Yankee Candle Store and something light and floral catches my interest at the Perfumery, but we don't slow. I turn toward the exit where I'd left Monty and my father sticks right with me. He pushes open the door and then we're outside in the steamy air and bright sunlight. The sky is darkening in the distance and thunder rumbles.

I unlock Monty and my father is in the passenger seat before I have my door closed.

"Drive," he instructs me.

With lack of further direction, I choose a route that heads further north along the U.S. highway that is the main thoroughfare just as it is in Seagate. I cross the bridge that spans the Orange River and hang a right. Eventually I can take another right and cross the old bridge which will take me into downtown Fort Dunn. I can wend my way through downtown and eventually end up back on the highway.

My father keeps an eye on the passenger side mirror almost the entire time. Occasionally he glances ahead or in my direction. Only once does he turn around. I pay closer attention to the rearview mirror since I assume he thinks we're being followed. I wonder if I'd be able to spot a tail. I know sometimes multiple cars are used to tail someone. The traffic is heavier than it was in Seagate and I can't determine if I see the same car behind me more than once.

Once we're downtown, he noticeably relaxes. He glances at me and I can tell he's looking at me and not out the window. "I would buy you lunch."

I glance over at him. It's like he read my mind.

"Near the mall," he says. "There is a very good Mexican restaurant."

"Iguana Mia." I smile.

We sit near the bar in a front corner window booth with a clear view of the both the restaurant entrance and most of the parking lot. He takes the seat with his back to the wall, of course.

I suppose there is a very good reason for the intrigue, the trek through downtown, his concern that we, or more likely he, might have been followed. But apparently he thinks we're safe enough to eat a meal in public, so I choose to ignore cloak and dagger business.

A dark-haired server takes my order for a Corona Light. Sasha, which is how I decide to think of him, orders Diet Coke with lime.

Our drinks arrive along with a basket of chips and salsa. I order without looking at the menu. Sasha orders fish tacos. I squeeze the lime into my beer and lift it in a toasting gesture toward him before I take a sip. Then I dive into the chips.

"You should not drink and drive," Sasha informs me.

"You don't get to tell me what to do." I try for a light tone, but it comes out sounding bitchy.

Sasha gracefully inclines his head to acknowledge the truth of my statement. He takes a sip from his glass and sets it down and watches while I devour some more chips and salsa.

"Don't you want any?"

"No, thank you."

"I was going to come here to eat anyway. Whether you showed up or not."

"You did not think I would?"

"Your track record of being there for me isn't the greatest."

Something flickers in his eyes. Again he does that sort of half-nod thing with his head, as if he's pleading no contest to the charge.

I drink more beer and eat more chips while he gazes out the window. I can't think of what to say to him. I already made my pitch about working with him to trap the Albanians and he basically blew me off. I'd all but thrown him out of my apartment the other night, but there were extenuating circumstances. Plus, he contacted me. It was up to him to tell me why.

Our food came. I order another beer and a glass of ice water. I cut into my chimichanga with relish.

Sasha has a refined way of eating with careful, precise movements as if he considers every bite before he puts it in his mouth. I can't tell if he is enjoying the food or he simply considers nourishment a necessity and it doesn't matter what's on his plate.

I drink about half of my second beer and eat most of my meal before I give up and sit back.

Sasha pushes his plate away and regards me for a moment. "I suppose you are wondering why I asked for this meeting."

"You didn't ask. You commanded."

He almost smiles, but he catches himself. The waitress comes to see if we need anything else and takes our plates away. "I think you have information that could be helpful to me."

"I didn't think you wanted my help. You keep warning me not to get involved."

"You do not listen to my warnings. Perhaps we can be of benefit to each other."

Now we're getting somewhere. Sasha is taking me seriously. If we're working together, I'll get to spend more time with him, get to know him, something I desperately want. I lean forward. "Tell me about The Millennium Project."

I'm pretty sure I surprised him.

"How do you know of that?"

"The Internet. Research." That is at least partially true. I don't want to begin a relationship with my father that's built on lies.

"What else do you know?" Now he is wary. Maybe even a little suspicious.

To make up for all the future lies I might be forced to tell him, I decide to lay most of my cards on the table right now.

The waitress comes back. "Can I get you anything else?" She wants to turn the table.

I dug a ten dollar bill out of my wallet. "Two coffees. We might be here for a little bit. She nods and goes away.

She came back in under a minute with two mugs of coffee, spoons, cream and sweeteners. "Enjoy!"

I ignore my coffee but Sasha takes a test sip of his.

I lean across the table again. "Here's what I know. The Espresso Mafia—"

"Who?" Sasha leans forward as if he couldn't hear me.

"The Albanians," I clarify.

"Why do you call them the Espresso, did you say? Mafia?"

He chuckles.

My hackles rise. "If you're just going to laugh at me, I'll be on my way." I put my napkin on the table and make as if to gather my purse and any other belongings I might have left, like I'm getting off an airplane or something.

"Tango. Please." He reaches toward me. "I mean no insult. It is a funny name you call them." He smiles and his face transforms. I can easily see how he charmed my mother and why she probably still has a thing for him.

"It's a joke," I admit.

"If joke, why are you upset if I laugh?"

"Because—" Lie only when necessary I remind myself. "I'm afraid you think I'm a joke. That you patronize me. Humor me. You don't take me seriously."

I pull my mug toward me and stare into it. Only my father can affect me this way. One minute I'm on top of the world and the next fear I might burst into tears.

"Tango," he says softly, urgently. "I do not laugh at you. I have not been a father to you, but you are my daughter. I want you only to be safe. Always."

"Okay." I take a sip of my coffee. It isn't bad. I decide to cut Sasha some slack. "Where I work that's what we call them. The Espresso Mafia. Because they travel in groups and they drink espresso. They don't seem to work but they always have a lot of money. They sit outside and smoke and drink coffee and act like they're God's gift to the world. They're disrespectful and they're slobs. I especially don't like their attitude toward women."

I sip some more coffee. Sasha listens.

"I saw a girl in the parking lot one night when I got off work. She was crying. She looked like someone beat her up. I spoke to her. She didn't want my help. She was pissed off but she was afraid, too. She was with one of the Albanians.

"At first I was just curious. I wanted to know how they could have so much money if they don't have jobs. Then I wanted to know what the deal was with the girl. I tried spying on them but that didn't work out so well. My friend Len—" I realize Sasha doesn't need to know names. "I found out there really is an Albanian Mafia and that they're operating here in the U.S. From what I read on the internet, they're brutal and clan-like and into all kinds of stuff. One of which is human trafficking. Another is prostitution.

"I went to a party in Royale Port and that same girl was there. She offered to do, uh, something sexual to my friend for a price. He declined but other guests at the party didn't.

"I tracked them to a house in Silvergate. I know there's a bunch of young girls living there, including the one I saw.

"I know the make, model and license plate number of at least one of the cars they drive. I know they have an abandoned house off Everglades Boulevard. I don't know what they use it for. To store guns maybe."

I sit back. Sasha had finished his coffee. "The house you mentioned where you think they store guns. You know where it is?"

I nod.

"An address?"

"Yes."

"What is it?"

"Not unless I go with you."

"Tango—"

"No. That's what you said. Maybe we can benefit each other. I want to put these guys away. *Badly*. It's what you want too. I've told you everything I know, well, almost everything. You've told me nothing."

Sasha sighs and shoves a hand through his hair. He looks at me across the table for a long moment before he reaches into a back pocket for his wallet. Our waitress appears with the check and he pays her in cash. He looks at me again. "You are many things, Tango. Passionate. Clever. Stubborn. Most definitely my daughter."

"You say that like it's a good thing." I hold my breath.

"It is."

Chapter Fifteen

Their deeds are bitter with poison

I am not terribly organized. After I work a shift, my apron goes into the bag I carry with me every day to Java Jake's and usually I don't switch aprons until one needs to be washed. Which is why the apron with the vial of forbidden coffee beans is still in my bag.

I remember it when I'm getting ready for bed. I retrieve the bottle and throw the apron in the dirty laundry. I need a place to hide my emergency cache of beans.

I wander around my apartment considering and rejecting possibilities. I don't want anyone else to discover them, but I need easy access to them. I stare at my jumbled mess of a closet. If I hide them in there I'll probably never find them. I reject the dresser drawers and anywhere in the kitchen as too obvious and easily accessible by someone other than me. There's no place in the living room/dining area combo, so that leaves the bathroom.

I turn on the light and stare at the narrow space. The small linen closet, vanity and toilet line the left side of the room with the tub at the end. I open the linen closet. Another jumbled mess, again too easily accessible. Same with the medicine cabinet. I glance above the vanity. The original fluorescent lighting is hidden behind a rectangular box-like structure covered with opaque plastic panels at the bottom. Updated lighting in the form of a strip of pewter pendant lights was added before I moved in. They'd left the fluorescent lights in the box and simply hung the pendants below it. As a result, there is a lot of light in my bathroom. The box gives me an idea. I step onto the closed toilet lid and from there to the vanity. I peek over the edge of the box. There is plenty of room to hide the bottle where no one will ever think to look. One of the back corners will be best. I reach to set the bottle in the left one and spot something else there. A small flat silver something.

I pick it up and stare at it. It's a flash drive. Odd. There are no markings on it. The business end of it is covered with a small clear plastic cap. I know what it is but how in the world had it gotten here? Why? Who?

It hasn't been here very long, either, because there is quite a coating of dust on the flat surfaces inside the box and even on the fluorescent tubes themselves. But not on the flash drive.

Weird. I have to remedy not having a computer soon. I can't take the jump drive to Cody or Lenny or anyone else and ask to use their computer. I can't risk using a library computer. Who know what's on it? I need a secure computer.

Listen to me. Like I really am a spy or something. A secure computer. Next I'll be scrambling calls and telling people to call me back on a burner phone. I smile to myself and decide I've chosen the best hiding place in my apartment. Someone else did too. I leave the beans and the flash drive side by side and go to bed.

Once there, though, I can't sleep. I lay awake building scenarios in my head about teaming up with my father to...what? Infiltrate the southwest Florida arm of the Albanian mob? To bring them down? To see justice done? To free those girls who I'm sure are being forced into prostitution?

I want it all but I have no idea how we'll go about it. Sasha made no guarantees or plans. I had the distinct feeling that he knows I can go places he can't. I have more freedom simply because I'm a free agent. It's possible his job with Interpol is merely to gather information and pass it on to whoever is in charge of the Millennium

Project. Maybe our agendas are entirely different. But that doesn't mean we can't be mutually beneficial to each other.

Information is power. Who said that? For some reason I think it was the character of Newman on an old episode of Seinfeld. The more information I acquire, the more power I'll have. The more I'll be able to share with Sasha. I'll prove my worth to him by finding out things and getting into places he can't.

All of a sudden it comes to me. I know who had hidden that jump drive. Sasha! The very first time he'd visited me. He asked to use the bathroom which had seemed a bit odd at the time. He hadn't seen me in over twenty years. He refused to even sit down, yet he'd used the bathroom. I don't know why he'd hidden it in my bathroom. I don't know what is on it. But I know that flash drive is his.

I flip back the covers and get dressed. I have a lot of black clothes because that's what I normally wear to work. Black shirts and pants and shoes. It's just after midnight when I creep out of my apartment as quietly as I can so as not to alert Cody. He might notice me firing up Monty but what I do and where I go isn't his business. *Unless you need him to rescue you.* I ignore my subconscious as best I can and slide behind the wheel.

I drive to Silvergate and cruise past the duplex where I know some of the Albanians reside. The silver Toyota is parked out front. Both sides of the duplex are dark.

It is possible that Albanians occupy the entire duplex. I've only been in one side, only seen them enter one side, but that doesn't mean anything. I haven't tracked their movements for any length of time, but this is as good a place as any to start.

The immediate neighborhood is an area in decline for the most part There are lots of small houses, duplexes and a few apartment buildings. The streets are narrow and there are no sidewalks. The poor lighting is a good thing as far as I'm concerned, but I need an inconspicuous place to park Monty.

Like my yellow Jeep, Monty sticks out like a sore thumb. He is big, black, shiny and memorable and obviously doesn't belong in this neighborhood where most of the vehicles are older model pickup trucks and cheap imports on their last legs.

The neighborhood is fairly quiet. I pass a few cars as I cruise the streets. Music blares from a couple of the residences and the occasional dog barks. A few teenagers congregate on the corners or shuffle along together on the side of the road.

Streetlights aren't plentiful and many are burnt out. Most of the streets have one at each corner and one in the middle.

I finally locate a place I think I can park Monty without a problem. It's an abandoned convenience store three streets away from the duplex. I noticed a clump of bushes across the street from the duplex that will provide cover for me. I figure I can crouch down there and watch the place for awhile without detection.

I turn Monty's engine off and locked the doors. As summer progresses into fall, the daily high temperature drops a few degrees and the nights are noticeably cooler, maybe in the low eighties. The unfamiliar darkened neighborhood gives me the creeps a little bit, but I reason no one knows I'm here, so the likelihood of a random attack is minimal.

Still, I keep my head down and skirt the couple of streetlights I pass, keeping to the shadows until I reach the unruly clump of bushes.

I honestly don't know what I think I'll discover. It's late. It's dark. There's little movement anywhere in the neighborhood. Yet I have to do *something* and this apparently is it.

I stand as close to the bushes as I can and fix my gaze on the dwelling across the street. If I dared to get closer would I detect anything going on inside? Just because it looks dark doesn't mean the occupants aren't awake. They could have blackout curtains. Maybe while I'm standing here those girls are being beaten or tortured or abused in a hundred ways I haven't thought of.

I can easily skirt the perimeter of the place without passing the front of it where the car is parked. I can listen, at least while I creep past one side, across the back and along the other side. Then I can hightail it back across the street and head for home. No one will know I was here. Not without lights on.

I glance around to make sure no one else is about. No cars had come down the street while I've been here. No doors opened, no one walked by.

I sprint across the street to the corner of the house and begin making my way along. There are two windows on this side, bedrooms probably. I stop next to each one and listen. The windows are closed, of course, because air conditioning is running. I hear nothing from inside so I move to the next corner and turn to make my way along the back of the house. I inch along, one hand on the stucco until I bump into a barrier. I hear a faint metal ping which makes me think of chain link fencing. I run my hand along a section in front of me to confirm my suspicion. Definitely a chain link fence. I reach up to discover it ends about six inches above my head which makes it six feet high.

It didn't occur to me to check out what was behind the duplex. I have my mini flashlight on my key ring but I really don't want to turn it on unless I absolutely have to. I step a few feet away from the house and let my fingers drift along the metal in search of a gate.

I don't know how, but I can tell from the narrow break in the fence and the thickness of the poles close together that I've found it. I use my sense of touch to find the hasp that keeps it closed. Carefully I lift it, push the gate open and step in, gently lowering the hasp. I can't do this in complete silence because of course there is a soft rasp of metal against metal, but I doubt it is loud enough to be heard inside. There's probably a gate on the other side as well, but if not, I assure myself I can retrace my steps and find this one.

I take one step in the direction of the house and hear a low growl. I freeze. I hear another one and rustling as of animal feet through grass.

I cross my arms over my chest and stand still as stone while two dogs snuffle and growl around me. I silently curse myself for my idiocy. How did it not occur to me to check out what was behind this duplex in the light of day before I came barreling out here in the dead of night?

Information is power I mimic myself. Yet I'd gone off on this ridiculous mission without nearly enough information and would now pay the consequences.

Why these two mongrels didn't bark before I even entered their domain I can't imagine. Perhaps they've been trained not to. Perhaps if they don't view me as a threat I'll be able to leave as quickly and as quietly as I arrived. Yeah, right, I chide myself. But isn't it worth a try?

I barely dare to breathe. I can feel their noses checking me out from my shoes to my crotch. They alternately growl and whine as if seeking answers about my presence here but not liking their own conclusions. Probably what they know for sure from their own instincts is that I don't belong here. I shouldn't be here. But what are they going to do about it?

I inch back toward the gate and they disapprove of that move based on the growls they emit. I can't stand here all night, though can I? If I wait them out will they lose interest?

I debate my options while they snuffle and growl. I can stand here indefinitely and hope they get tired of sniffing and growling, but then what? Eventually I'll have to move. I have to try to get back through the gate. Without them.

Even if the dogs start barking during my escape attempt, if I get through the gate without them and run, no one will know it was me they were barking at, right? Right?

My only problem is, even though I'm not that far from the gate, I need to know exactly where the hasp is. I won't have time to fumble for it, not with these two tracking my every move. The image of each of them taking a nice big bite out of me is all I can think about. I oh so carefully slide one hand down and into my pocket. My keys jangle against each other as I pull them free. One of the dogs gives a soft huffing bark at the noise. I hold my breath and wait for a light to come on inside. Or outside for that matter. Why didn't I reconnoiter this whole scene in daylight? There is probably a back door, a stoop, a patio, a table, chairs, and a hose. There could be a clothesline, a doghouse, and a kiddie pool, for all I know. There could be any number of obstacles waiting to trap me or trip me up in the dark.

No light comes on. I maneuver my keys, keeping my hand up near my chest because the last thing I want to do is have the jaws of one of those dogs clamped around my hand. I have a feeling they are the type who won't let go once they decide to take a bite of something. Or someone.

Ever so slowly, excruciatingly slowly so as not to alarm the dogs I turn myself around so I'm facing the fence. They stop growling but they don't relax. They circle me, keeping me under guard.

I take a couple of slow, deep breaths to steady myself. As soon as I flash my mini light and locate the hasp on the gate I'm going to make a run for it. I have to hope, since these dogs didn't attack me upon my arrival that they are trained only to sound an alert when necessary and not to do damage that can't be repaired. The gate wasn't locked. If they were truly dangerous, wouldn't it be?

Then again, these are the Albanians I'm dealing with. I doubt they'd care if dogs attack an intruder on their premises. For all I know there are warnings posted along the fence. *Bad dog. Keep out.* If I'd done my homework in the light of day, I'd know all about the fence and what was inside it.

When you control the *mail* you control information. That's what Newman had said in that Seinfeld episode. I don't know why it came to me at that exact moment, but it did.

I can beat myself up more about my lapse in preplanning later. Right now I have to get the hell out of here. *No guts no glory.* I raise my key ring and depress the button for the light. It flashes on the gate. I locate the hasp at the same moment the dogs start barking. Startled, I fumble the keys as I take my first step toward freedom.

The light goes out. I grasp at the air with both hands, but I can't catch the keys before they hit the ground. I barrel blindly toward the gate anyway, shove the hasp up and fall through it. I hear the rip of material and realize one of the dogs has the cuff of my pants in his teeth. I close the gate on my leg as I try to tug my pants out of his mouth. The other dog's teeth clamp on the toe of my sneaker. His teeth slide through the canvas and hit my toes.

In a panic I kick and tug realizing it is just as I thought. Once they sink their teeth in, they don't to let go. Dog number one succeeds in ripping the piece of material off my pants. He falls back with his prize. Without the pressure of him holding my leg down, I kick out at dog number two. I might have yanked his teeth out. I hear another ripping sound and then both dogs start barking in earnest. I cling to the fence to keep myself upright as I regain my balance. With shaky fingers I replace the hasp on the closed gate.

I don't have my keys but I escaped with my life. I'll worry about my keys later. A light comes on and illuminates a small patch of the back yard. I whirl and run back the way I came along the side of the house.

I hear shouts in a foreign language from the backyard. Albanian? Maybe. I don't stop to listen or analyze. I reach the front corner, glance once over my shoulder and ram into something that drops me in my tracks.

Chapter Sixteen

They act like men of Sodom and Gomorroah

I come to with a bright light shining directly in my eyes. I am tightly strapped to a chair with what looked like those heavy duty straps used in moving vans to keep things from shifting. They are a bit like faded yellow seatbelts. There is one across my upper body, one around my waist and another restrains my thighs. My wrists are bound with those little plastic straps the cops used. Zip ties I think they're called. Seriously? I'm a cliché of every movie I've ever seen when the bad guys want to interrogate somebody they believe is threatening their organization.

I close my eyes against the light but not before I get a sense of the situation. Indoors, for sure. The air is stifling, musty and stale. The odor of lots of dust. Perspiration roll off my skin and my clothes are stuck to me. The edges of the strap across my upper body dig painfully into my biceps. I catch a glimpse of a concrete floor and concrete block walls. A garage, perhaps. Or a warehouse of some kind. I think of the abandoned house off Everglades Boulevard. My sense, however, is that this is a much larger place.

I open my eyes again when I hear the murmur of voices. Albanian, I think. At this point I should recognize the language even if I can't understand what is being said. I turn away from the light, squinting into the darkness. Footsteps. A door opens and closes. I sense them approaching. I practice deep breathing. I'll stay calm no matter what. My mantra is, *I'm not dead yet.* As long as I'm alive I have a chance to survive whatever these guys have in mind.

"Miss Rutledge, why do you not listen to our previous warnings? Why do you continue to, how do you say? Peek your nose in?"

I cock my head to one side. This is not a voice I've heard previously in connection to the Albanians.

When I don't answer, the voice continues. "What am I to do with you?"

What an odd interrogation. Nothing but rhetorical questions.

"There are, among my associates, those who have suggested the simplest method of eliminating your interference is to kill you. But I fear you have too many friends with whom you may have shared your suspicions. Friends who would ask too many questions. Perhaps friends who, like you, show too much interest in my business.

"Torture?" He lets that idea hang out there for several seconds.

You had me at kill, I think wildly. Visions of severed fingers, broken kneecaps and facial disfigurement fill my head. My perspiration rate increases right along with my heart rate.

"Personally, I have no stomach for it," he goes on in that same conversational tone. "The same cannot be said for several of my associates, however. They would be quite...interested in having their way with you. I have personal knowledge of their creativity in such endeavors. Extracting information from one unwilling to part with it is a particular specialty of theirs. I daresay the more unwilling the participant the more my associates enjoy their work." A few seconds pass before he asks a question I think he honestly wants me to answer. "Who are you working for?"

"Java Jake's."

"I do not like these games you play." He no longer seems amused. I hear footsteps as though he is pacing in the shadows to my left. I turn my head but see only what appears to be a blurry outline of a possible human form. I can't be sure I see anyone.

"Do you recall a flower delivery you received recently?" He pauses. "The delivery man is especially adept at extracting information from individuals such as yourself."

Delivery man. Interesting job title. What he delivered to me was a beating plain and simple. Plus a warning. *Go back to pouring coffee. Be a good girlie or you and that boyfriend of yours won't like what happens next.*

That beating and the warning had the opposite effect, making me even more determined to find out what the Albanians are up to here in Seagate. I'll be damned if I'll let them push me around. I'd told myself I'd be smarter about spying on them, but I had a lot to learn. I'd been "peeking my nose in" and leaving quite an impression.

While I was deep breathing trying to stay calm, I listened, not just to the voice of my interrogator, but to any other sounds I could hear. I hoped to get clues to where I am, to gather some intel on these Albanians and what they are doing. Unfortunately, not much sound penetrated the concrete block walls, other than the rumble of something mechanical outside. Certainly not an air conditioner. A generator perhaps.

"I will ask you once more. Who are you working for?"

"No one."

I sense my answer displeases him. If I tell him the truth, I have a feeling he won't believe me. He doesn't say anything, but the energy in the room shifts. I can feel his frustration. In a small separate part of myself I wonder what kind of torture I'll be subjected to. Another beating? A severed pinky finger? Waterboarding?

"Ah. You want to protect your associates just as I do. However, you will soon learn, as I have, that with loyalty comes a price tag. You have been warned, Miss Rutledge. More than once, as I'm sure you realize. You are foolish, but hardly a threat. Yet. Hardly worth my time or notice. However, there is another American saying. Curiosity killed the kitten? Perhaps you have heard of it?"

"The cat," I murmur.

"What was that?"

I raise my voice. "Curiosity killed the cat. Not the kitten."

His laughter bounces around the room and off the concrete. There is nothing sinister in it. He sounds genuinely full of glee as if he's never heard anything so entertaining as me correcting him.

"Ah, Miss Rutledge," he says, once he stops laughing. "At last I understand your appeal. I am rarely so amused. It would sadden me greatly to have you permanently dealt with."

His tone changes. "But know this: at the slightest indication that it becomes necessary, I will indeed give such an order. Your Jeep won't be the only thing they'll find in a canal."

I hear a door open and close. Relief swamps me. Does that mean, as I hope, that my execution is off the table? At least for the time being?

I hear muffled voices, one in particular. His? raised over the others who seem to be asking questions. The door opens again. At least two sets of footsteps approach. Something slips over my head and drops to my collar bone. If feels like heavy cloth. I can hardly breathe, but I fight the urge to whimper. The last thing I want to do is show weakness to any of these guys. I concentrate on breathing as best I can. The cloth is loose although the temperature surrounding my head soars another ten degrees.

The straps holding me are released and I'm pulled roughly to my feet. "Walk!" comes the curt order. I'm seized by a strong hand around each bicep, one guy on either side of me. I stumble between them but my slight weight has no impact on their balance. They drag-carry me through the door, down a corridor, through another door which leads outside. I am tossed into the back of what must be a van. My knees and hip bone bounce off the ridged metal floor. The double door slam and I hear the scrape of a key turning a lock. I manage to scramble upright to a seated position, my back against the side of the van, as the engine roars to life and we start to move. The van jolts over rough terrain, hits several dips, bouncing me up and down on the metal floor.

I pray for air conditioning, but there doesn't seem to be any. The back of the van is apparently closed off from the front because I can't hear, smell or even sense my handlers. In spite of my interrogator's reassurance I wonder if they'll take me somewhere and kill me. I try to think how I might avoid it. My wrists are still bound so tightly the plastic is digging into my flesh. I might not be bleeding, but a bit more pressure would do the trick. They didn't bind my ankles, though, so if I can get free somehow, I can at least run. Except I still have the covering over my head. I lift my wrists and explore the cloth. I try to lift it, but it's secured somehow at the back so I can't draw it above my chin. I pull the material as far away from my nose as I can to get the most air. Little butterfly wings of panic try to work their way up from my gut but I beat them back. Panic is the enemy. I have to think. I'd been dumb enough not to plan ahead and dumb enough to get caught. Now I have to be smart. Operating on the assumption that I am in an enclosed space and my captors can't see me, I push myself up to stand. I brace myself with my forearms against the ceiling and my feet wide apart. The van takes a turn onto a smoother road. I listen for sounds of other traffic, trying to get a sense of our location, but I can't detect much. Periodically the van slows, stops, then accelerates. After a bit I can hear the occasional sounds of traffic nearby. Are we heading back into town instead of away from it? The thought gives me hope. Surely, if they plan to kill me, they'll do it somewhere private. They can dump my body in a canal off Everglades Boulevard and there is a good chance no one will ever find me. Not if the alligators get to me first.

Whatever they have planned, I decide I'm not going down without a fight. I maneuver around to the double doors. I try the handles, but they are locked. I use them as hand holds. I figure that way I'll know the second they unlock them. I'll come out fighting, kicking, whatever it takes. If I can catch them off guard I might be able to get away. Even with my wrists bound and my eyes covered, I might be able to outrun them.

My interrogator thinks I'm a fool. That I'm not a threat. Oh, yeah? Want to bet? Intellectually I know it's better if he doesn't consider me a threat. But I don't care for being thought an idiot by him or anyone else. Mostly what my capture and subsequent interrogation did is piss me off and insult me. There is something reminiscent in the way my father treats me at times. With a mixture of condescension, disbelief and grudging admiration. What I want is respect. Not only from my father and but from whoever is in charge of this crew of Albanians. I want to be taken seriously.

The van slows and turns a couple of times in quick succession. My muscles are a bit shaky from the effort of bracing myself to keep from losing my balance and the anticipation of what I need to do once the van stops.

It happens sooner than I expect. The gears shift. The driver's and passenger doors open. I hear the crunch of footsteps in gravel on either side. Adrenaline streaks through me. A key slides into the door lock,. There's the sound of metal on metal and the click of the released locking mechanism. The handles turn downward beneath my hands. Suddenly, I know what to do. I crouch slightly and put all my weight into shoving the doors outward. I hear them impact on the two guys, solid thuds of metal against bodies and then I'm out. I fall and hit the ground hard, practically landing flat on my hooded face. I scramble up, poise to run, but meaty fingers wrap around my ankle. I kick out at the same time the fingers tug on my ankle. I fall with an "Oof!" to the ground. Adrenaline and my need to keep fighting make me kick out with my other foot. I think I hear a chuckle from one of them. He tries to grab me, but I kick blindly and connect with something. A shin perhaps. I feel the impact of it shudder all the way up my leg and there's a grunt of surprise from the number two guy. A low stream of Albanian follows which might be curse words or instructions to the guy who still holds my ankle.

I continue to writhe and kick and try to get away. I hear more grumbling before everything goes black.

Chapter Seventeen

Of all the slain and captives,

I rise to consciousness this time surrounded by darkness. Rain patters down on me from a starless sky. I sit up slowly and notice a variety of discomforts emanating from various parts of my body. My jaw, my wrists, my toes, my limbs. I am in a patch of gravelly grass. I can make out a dark, shiny shape next to me. I reach out to steady myself against it and get to my feet. *Monty?* No way.

Had those goons dropped me back at my car right where I'd left it a couple of streets over from the house in Silvergate?

The rain came down harder. I pat my pockets to discover before I remember I don't have my keys. I round the car, knowing it's locked. I try the door handle anyway. It isn't locked. I slide onto the passenger seat. My derriere connects with something sharp. My keys! I can't believe it. I've been chased by dogs, kidnapped and interrogated. But my captors returned me to my vehicle *and* left my keys. Unbelievable. I glance at myself in the rear view then pull down the visor to check for facial damage. My jaw looks a little puffy. I run my fingertips along it and move my facial muscles experimentally. I know why everything went black. Twice.

I stare at my wrists. Those plastic zip ties left angry red welts around both wrists. Those will be hard to hide. Exhaustion swamps me. I start Monty's engine and drive home.

I swim up from a deep sleep filled with troubling dreams I don't want to remember. Somebody is knocking on my door, but it takes me a few minutes to make sense of the fact that the knocking is not part of a dream.

I lift my head from the pillow about the time the knocking stops. I let my head drop back to the pillow grateful that whoever was knocking gave up.

"Tee? You in here?"

"Yeah," I call back. My voice is weak and raspy. I clear my throat and sit up just as Cody pokes his head through my bedroom door. He stares at me, his gaze clouding as he gives me a professional once over, sizing up the situation. Still covered by the sheet and my nightshirt, I bring my knees up to my chest and clasp my hands around them. I can sense his teeth sinking into his tongue as he refrains from saying whatever it is he wants to say. I hate every second of it.

I wait until I can't stand the silence between us any longer. I keep my gaze on his. "Can we make a deal? You say whatever you want, ask me whatever you want. If I can't tell you the truth, I'll just tell you I can't give you an answer."

"Deal. What happened to you?" He step closer to the bed and puts a finger under my chin. His thumb brushes along my jaw. I flinch a little. He picks up my wrist and looks at it. His expression darkens. "Did Joe do this to you?"

"No!"

"The Espresso Mafia?" He lifts a brow, which to me means he still thinks the Espresso Mafia is this big joke.

"I can't give you an answer," I tell him sulkily. I've stupidly boxed myself in by making that earlier deal with him. In trying to salvage our friendship by keeping some semblance of honesty between us, I gave him the ability to get information simply by my refusal to answer any question.

"Great. That's just great." He turns for the door. "Get dressed. I'm buying breakfast."

After he leaves and tugs the door closed behind him, I scramble out of bed. I grab clothes and in the bathroom I strip down and examine my appearance. I have a few bruises on my arms and legs. Nothing major. My wrists are rubbed raw by those damn plastic ties. My jaw is a little puffy and has a dark red tinge to it. My toes have tiny puncture wounds, but mostly my feet were protected by my shoes and socks.

I get myself together, and use some foundation to cover my puffy jaw. I mascara my lashes and dab on some shadow hoping that will serve as a distraction from my other injuries. I put on black shorts and a white camisole along with a sheer white long-sleeved shirt. I leave it mostly unbuttoned in deference to the summer heat. The cuffs cover my wrists.

We take Cody's car, a three-year-old Honda Accord coupe, to the Sunrise Diner. We ride in silence. We both need coffee before conversation.

I perk up after a few sips to discover that apparently, abduction is good for the appetite. I'm starving. But that might be because I haven't eaten since lunch yesterday. I order French toast and bacon and pretend my morning is starting now.

"What happened at the hearing?" I'm glad to see that the injuries Randall Grimes inflicted on Cody are almost completely healed.

"I'm in the clear." Cody sips his pale beige coffee. "I was on my way to the ER when he died. My testimony didn't help anyone.

"It didn't hurt anyone, either, though, did it?"

"I guess not. Look, Tee, your Jeep was found yesterday."

I stare at Cody. *Your Jeep won't be the only thing they'll find in a canal.* "In a canal?" I've had so much else occupying my mind, that comment by my captor didn't register until now.

Cody stares back at me, a glimmer of suspicion in his gaze. "How'd you know?"

"I—I didn't. I had sort of a premonition, I guess you'd say. It was just a hunch. About the canal."

Cody continues to regard me. I know he doesn't believe me.

"Where was it?" I ask.

"Oh, you mean that wasn't part of your 'hunch'?"

"Nope," I say easily. "Just that it might be in or near a canal."

"Couple of guys from the water management district were doing a routine inspection in the northeast quadrant. Noticed the roll bar and called it in."

"You mean it was completely submerged?"

"I guess it had been. You know how full the canals get in the summer. But the water tables are down. I just happened to hear about it yesterday when I stopped by the station. You'll probably get a call about it later."

"It's totaled anyway," I say glumly, "if it's been in the water that long." I'd loved my Jeep. Even if it did stand out when I tried to trail the Espresso Mafia.

"You got the insurance money. Plus you got Monty." Cody grins.

"Correction. The bank got the insurance money."

"But you still got Monty." Cody sips his coffee. "Anyway, they're going to haul it out of the canal this afternoon. If you want to be there, I'll go with you."

I can't imagine what being submerged in a canal has done to the Jeep. Images of mud and slime come to mind. I had a lot of memorable times in the Jeep. My first date with Joe for one. The Espresso Mafia was responsible for destroying the first vehicle I'd owned. A line from a movie or somewhere popped in my head: *Now it's personal.* They'd hurt Lenny. They'd hurt me. I knew they were hurting those young women.

But I feel violated in a way I didn't before because now I know for sure it was them. They'd taken something I loved and destroyed it. They'd sent me a message. This time it was some*thing*. The next time it would be some*one*.

A slow roll of anger burns through me. If they had a fight it was with me. If they wanted to hurt me by hurting what I cared about, by God I'd find what *they* cared about and I'd destroy it. With or without help, I swore I'd bring them down. By the time I got done with whatever it was I ended up doing, they'd be begging for mercy.

"Thanks, Cody. I would like to be there."

The server brought our order. The news about the Jeep coupled with my memory of last night's events, culminating with the insinuation that I might also meet my end in a canal did little to dim my appetite.

Chapter Eighteen

For he will avenge his people,

By the time Cody and I arrive on the scene there is a big flatbed tow truck, a patrol unit and a dark blue sedan parked along the dirt road bordering the canal. We're on the outskirts of Colfax County, quite close to the Everglades.

The canals here are deeper and wider than the ones in the populated areas.

As soon as Cody and I get out of the car the door of the sedan pops open and a guy I'd have known was a cop even if he didn't have a badge and a sidearm, gets out and starts toward us. He is fiftyish with a tough guy build and a Marine haircut. He wears aviator sunglasses, a white, short-sleeved dress shirt with the sleeves rolled up to show off his biceps, and a dark blue tie.

"Cavallaro?"

"Yes, sir." He and Cody shake hands.

"Miss Rutledge." He nods at me but something make me think he is critically appraising me behind those dark lenses. "Detective Perry Hanson."

I open my mouth to ask why a detective is interested in the recovery of my Jeep, but I decide better of it. Detective Hanson doesn't miss my decision to keep my mouth shut, however.

He turns to move closer to where two burly tow truck guys are evaluating the situation. Cody and I follow. The cop from the patrol unit is stationed near the tow truck. He and Cody nod at each other. "What can you tell me about the theft of your vehicle, Miss Rutledge?" Hanson asks in a conversational tone.

"Isn't everything already in the report?"

Cody nudges me at the same time I see Hanson's jaw tighten.

"I don't know what more I can tell you," I add with that sulky tone in my voice.

"Know anyone who's got a grudge against you?" Hanson asks.

We stop walking to gaze at the scene before us. I can see the top of the Jeep and a sliver of the rear window. The tow truck guys have flipped a coin. The loser gets the job of wading into the canal to attach the winch. They look like identical twins whose older brother might be Larry the Cable Guy.

I fold my arms across my chest. I'm not prepared for the sight of my beloved Jeep dead from drowning. Patrick's attachment to Monty doesn't seem so ridiculous now. I blink rapidly behind my sunglasses and try to take a deep breath. Cody's comforting hand on the back of my neck almost pushes me over the edge.

"Miss Rutledge?" Hanson prompts.

I can't stop staring at what I can see of the Jeep. I don't trust myself to speak so I shake my head.

"No one?" he presses. "Somebody you might have pissed off? A relationship that ended badly? Anyone in your life looking for revenge?"

I shake my head more vigorously. I can feel tears pressing into my eyes. A lump settles in my throat. What if the next time it isn't my car that ends up in the canal? What if it's someone I love?

"Why do you ask?" Cody asks.

Hanson turns to face us. His gaze bores into me. I lift my chin and uncross my arms. I'm not helpless and I'm not going to let him think I am. Cody is there for moral support but I can handle this detective.

He says, "Usually there's a reason someone steals a car. They've committed a crime and need a getaway vehicle. Kids looking for a joy ride. Cars are stolen, shipped out of the country and sold. Maybe they're torn apart for parts."

Hanson and I stare at each other from behind our sunglasses before he continues. "But that didn't happen here. Somebody stole your car and dumped it in a canal. Somebody wanted to send you a message." Hanson's gaze flickers to Cody then back to me.

"What message is it you think they're sending?"

"That the next time we find something in a canal it won't be your car."

Hanson pivots and walks off to stand next to the patrol deputy. The losing tow truck guy is wet and muddy but the winch is in reverse and inch by inch the Jeep crawls backwards up the incline. Water sluices out of the open windows and from below the doors.

I cover my mouth with my hand as my stomach clenches and I taste my breakfast in the back of my throat. Cody slides his hand around mine and I hold on, willing myself to maintain control. "You okay?" he says.

I nod unable to look away from my waterlogged Jeep. When it's entirely out of the canal, the momentum of the winch stops while water continues to drain.

I can't hear what the four men are discussing amongst themselves. I edge closer and Cody comes with me. The sun beat down on us. I am past thinking I might cry and am now perspiring profusely. We all are.

Hanson glances over his shoulder just as I lift my arm to blot the sweat from my forehead. The unbuttoned cuff of my shirt falls away. His gaze locks on the abraded area around my wrist. He frowns before turning his attention back to the recovery process.

Eventually the Jeep makes its way onto the flatbed of the tow truck. The patrol cop drives off and so does the truck. Hanson makes his way over to us. "I might need to speak with you again, Miss Rutledge. Tie up any loose ends."

I nod. "Has this ever happened before?" My voice is shaky and I do my best to make it stronger. "Where somebody stole a car and just dumped it for no apparent reason?"

"In the last couple of years, yeah it's happened a couple of times. Never had any solid leads, though. Of course, after the bodies were discovered in the same general area, I had to turn the cases over to Homicide."

"Bodies?" I whisper.

"Owners of the vehicles. That's why I asked if anyone had a grudge against you. Maybe someone's sending you a warning."

Be a good girlie. Go back to selling coffee.

"Here's my card," Hanson say holding one out to me. I take it. "You call me if you think of anything." He nods to Cody, gets into his unmarked sedan and leaves. Cody and I trudge back to his car. I have to give Cody credit. He doesn't say a word.

Chapter Nineteen

No wonder we are afraid of you!

I delay as long as I can at work the next day before I sneak into the storeroom and lock it behind me. Skulking. That's what I'm doing. I don't have much time. I'd counted out of the safe and the crew chief coming on is occupied counting in.

I hurriedly pull syrup bottles off the shelf and find my bag of beans. I retrieved one, taking just a second to look at it closely before popping it in my mouth. I can't even enjoy the ritual any more. I know the coating won't last long enough for me to identify it. The romance of the beans is over. They are a necessity now, like air or water. I need them to survive...as me.

I hide them again and replace everything and slide back into the role of Tee Rutledge, Assistant Store Manager Java Jake's Store #1284.

After I clock out I discover I a text message from Joe. He has a dinner meeting tonight but do I want to meet him for a drink? I certainly do. I text him back and we agree on a meeting place. The Pub on Fifth Avenue.

When I walk out of Java Jake's I discover Lenny waiting for me, nursing the last of his iced coffee. He drops the cup into the trash bin and falls into step next to me. "We need to talk."

I don't argue with him. In truth, even though I am concerned for his safety, I am ridiculously glad to see him. And I'm even happier that he looks none the worse for wear after his "accident." The odd pitter-patter of my heart is not quite the same as it is when I see Joe. But there's definitely something there. Something I'd prefer not to acknowledge. I initially put Lenny into the friend category and I'd like him to stay there.

He guides me to a silver Mercedes sedan and opens the passenger door for me. "You're kidding, right?"

"It's my Mom's car. There's a bit of a hold-up with my insurance company."

I got in trying not to think too much about the fact that my car and Lenny's truck were both totaled in the last couple of weeks. "Where are we going?"

"Nowhere. I want to talk to you where we can't be overheard."

He exits the parking lot and heads west on Pine Ridge Road.

"How are you Lenny? You look great." I don't know if Lenny is making an effort to mainstream himself, but something is definitely different. His clothes fit better. His hair isn't quite as crazy. I can't tell if he's added any new tattoos.

He grins at the compliment. I've never thought of Lenny as being all that attractive, but when he smiles, it transforms his features. And now that know him better, his personality definitely makes him more attractive to me. And then there's the memory of that one kiss we shared—

I call a halt to my thoughts. Lenny is a friend. That is all.

"I did some more checking," he says.

"Lenny." I told him to stop researching the Albanians. What am I supposed to do? I can't stop him. I can only warn him. I turn to look at him while he drives. He has a strong profile I never noticed before. A determined chin. He might be out of the mainstream, but he isn't stupid.

"Strakosha owns a whole lot of stuff," he goes on, as if I hadn't spoken. "Restaurants, mostly, which makes sense. It's an easy way to launder money. He's invested in a bunch of real estate, too. Another easy way to hide money. I've run down a list of properties he owns under different company names.

"You're not going to stop, are you?"

He glances at me at a stop light. "Are you?"

I look away. Out the front window. To the side. I take in the other cars, the sunlight glancing off their hoods and roofs. Life going on as usual in Seagate. The light turns and we started moving. "I don't want anything to happen to you."

"Aww, Tee. Careful now or I'll think you have a soft spot for me."

He is teasing but I do have a soft spot for him. I know instinctively, Lenny is one of those guys who will always have my back. Loyal to a dangerous fault. He'll risk his own safety to protect someone he cares about. He cares about me and I've foolishly put him in harm's way. And now I can't keep him out of it.

"They found my Jeep."

"Where?"

"In a canal. There was a detective there when they pulled it out. He wanted to know if I'd made any enemies."

"Of course you told him nothing."

"Lenny..." I rub my fingers across my forehead hoping that will help me think of what I want to say. What I need to say.

Lenny pulls into the parking lot of one of the public beaches. He gets out so I follow him to the concession stand. We get cups of soft serve ice cream and take seats at the nearly deserted covered pavilion.

"Your accident. My Jeep. Those were warnings."

"Of course."

"You don't seem too concerned about it. These guys, Lenny, maybe right now they don't think we're much of a threat."

"Because they haven't killed us yet, you mean?" Lenny smiles when he says it, like this is all some kind of joke.

"Dammit, Lenny!" I shove my cup of ice cream away. "I don't want anything to happen to you. Not because of me."

He frowns. "That's all you care about? You don't care if I'm dead so long as nothing you did caused it."

"That's not what I meant."

"That's what it sounds like."

"I don't want you dead at all. Whether it's because of me or not."

"Good." He goes back to his ice cream.

I'm not conveying my frustration with him very well. "I don't know what to do with you."

He waggles his brows. "I've got a couple of suggestions if you—"

I throw a crumpled napkin at him. "Stop it. You know what I mean."

He pushes his ice cream cup away and leans across the table. "Look, Tee, there's something going on in this town that I don't like. This Albanian group seems to have crept in under the radar and they're spreading their influence. It may have started with those girls at my parents' party. That's what started it for me, anyway. I didn't like what was going on, but there's so much more to their operation than a prostitution ring. And this Nickolai Strakosha is at the head of it."

I suppose if I can't stop Lenny, I can accept whatever information he uncovered. That doesn't mean I have to tell him anything that I know which might only increase the risk for him.

I know I can't control Lenny. "We should leave this to the authorities," I say.

"Is that what you're going to do?"

"I don't want you involved!" I cry. "Don't you get it? They'll kill you Lenny. And your death will be just one more thing they won't be held accountable for."

"And you think it will be your fault."

"I don't want anything else to happen to you."

"Got it. Now what's our next move?"

Lenny is as stubborn as I am. Blithely ready to carry on in spite of the risks. He reminds me of my father. But my father got smart. He figured out a way to operate under the Albanians' radar. Or so it appears. That's what Lenny and I need to do.

"Our next move is to stay alive and not get caught."

At five-thirty I enter The Pub and give myself a second so that my eyes can adjust to the dim lighting. I don't see Joe anywhere so I make my way to the bar and find an empty stool. The place is fairly crowded for mid-week. Guys in suits with loosened ties and pretty women in office attire.

As usual, I second-guess my outfit choice. I'm sure my cotton skirt and simple top and sandals brand me as non-executive material. The welts on my wrists have faded, but I cleverly cover them up with a wristwatch on one and a bracelet on the other. I get a glimpse of myself in the mirror behind the bar. My makeup looks pretty good. I almost have that smoky eye thing down. So I smile at myself. A bartender smiles back and sets a napkin out. "What'll it be?"

I need something I can sip while I wait for Joe. Plus I have to drive myself home. "A glass of wine."

"Red? White?"

"White. Pinot grigio if you have it."

"Sure thing."

"Here alone?" A thirty-something executive type sidles up next to me.

"I'm meeting someone," I tell him coolly.

"Please tell me it's a girlfriend. Or your mother."

I smile because I find the idea that the guy is maybe hitting on me amusing. "No."

"Damn."

"I'm Kevin Bartlett. Like the pear." He holds out his hand.

I raise an eyebrow. "Do you always introduce yourself that way?"

"I do actually," he says, finally relinquishing my hand. My wine appears and I take a sip. "It's like Fat Amy in Pitch Perfect. I say it before someone else does. 'Oh, like the pear?' I've heard that all my life. Might as well get it out of the way up front."

"How...refreshing." Kevin Barlett isn't bad looking. I peg him for a broker. Or a banker based on the dark blue pin-striped suit and the red tie with a small pattern.

"And you are?"

"A fascinating woman who shouldn't be kept waiting." Joe presses his lips against my temple. "Excuse us," he says to Kevin.

"Sure thing." Kevin disappears into the crowd.

"I can't leave you alone for two seconds, can I?" Joe grins when he says it. I smile back. My heart does that pitter-pat racing thing it always does when I'm with Joe. He'd gone all possessive on me and that thrills me.

"You know I always have to have one or two guys waiting in the wings just in case."

"In case of what?" he signals to the bartender. "Stella." He turns his attention back to me.

"In case you leave me hanging."

"Never." He leans in and kisses me lightly on the lips. Heaven.

"Tell me about your day," I say. Anything so long as I don't have to tell him about mine.

Joe looks taken aback. "Seriously? You're asking about my day?"

"Is that wrong? Am I not supposed to?" I lean in. "Are you a spy or something? Working undercover? Have I compromised you?"

Joe raises his glass of beer and appraises me with a twinkle in his eye. "Not yet."

"I'm just surprised," he says, after he sets his glass back on the bar. "That's usually my line. And once I ask..."

"Then what happens?"

"We spend the rest of the evening talking about...never mind." He drinks some more beer.

"How's Scorch?" I say. At least his cat is something we have in common and a safe enough subject.

"He's getting so big. You should come over and visit him. I think he misses you." Joe reaches for my hand and rubs his thumb along the back of it. My stomach does a flip-flop. "I miss you. I could cook you dinner one night next week? How about that?"

"I thought you couldn't cook."

"I can order takeout and we can eat at my house one night next week. How about that?"

"Chinese?"

"Perfect."

"And Scorch will be there to chaperone."

"Oh, I don't think we'll need a chaperone."

Chapter Twenty

Taking vengeance on his enemies,

It's cool and wet and humid. I can smell the wet earth beneath me, but I can't see it even though I'm pretty sure my eyes are open. Wherever I am it's dark and close. I feel surrounded. I stretch a hand out in the darkness and discover it's not exactly a hand. Or at least it doesn't feel like my hand. But I contact something soft yet solid. The ground beneath me?

I wiggle around a bit, but I am somehow contained. My body feels weirder than it has ever felt. It's hard describe, but it's almost like I'm enclosed. It's disconcerting and a little frightening. If only I could see!

I wiggle and push and try to orient myself and suddenly my head pops out of whatever it is that surrounds me and I take a breath of the fresh, wet night air. I blink, but I still can't see all that well, perhaps because it's dark and evidently I am on the ground.

I have legs of a sort at least even if I don't have hands. I somehow can dig my legs in the ground and turn myself around to try to get a handle on where I am. What I am is going to be a bit more difficult.

It isn't that easy to see, but once I've about-faced I do see light coming from a house. It illuminates a manicured lawn which I am at the far end of. There is what looks like a screened deck at the back of the house. My range of vision is not that great but maybe because it's so far away it makes it easier to see.

I take a couple of test steps. Surprisingly, I can move fairly well along the ground through the grass. I can't really feel it beneath me except for where my feet hit it and then it's more of a sensation of sinking into the wet earth and the grass swishing beneath me.

I think maybe I am in the body of a turtle because I can't think of anything else that would move this way. Am I a box turtle? Or maybe a gopher tortoise. Chances of me seeing anything about my current body are nonexistent. I can only turn my head so far and in the darkness I can't see much except the lights ahead of me.

I head that way. I move fairly well and quickly cover the lawn until I am at the base of the deck. I could crawl under it but there seems no point. In fact, I'm not sure why I'm here or what to do. Continue to wander around?

While I'm contemplating my next move I hear a door above me open and footsteps cross the deck. The door closes and I hear the scrape of chairs.

"Nice place you've got here, Nicky."

I suck in a breath. I know that voice. It's Joe.

"It is adequate," comes the accented reply from another male. I cock my head concentrating on the accent. I don't think it's Albanian but something about it strikes a familiar note. This was Joe's dinner meeting?

Joe laughs. "I'd say it's better than 'adequate.'"

So would I if I had the ability. The deck overlooks another lower deck. I don't know what's up there but if I had to guess, probably an outdoor bar, a seating area, possibly a hot tub.

"It is a matter of opinion, is it not? I am interested in perhaps purchasing a home in Heritage Bay."

"There will be some beautiful homes, there," Joe agrees.

"I have retained a lovely real estate agent, also. Sammi Rutledge. Do you know her?"

"I do actually."

I wait for Joe to explain that he'd been dating me, Sammi's sister.

"As you Americans say, she is one hot mama. I am tempted to mix business with pleasure."

"Good luck," Joe says. I wonder what he means by that. Evidently his companion does as well.

"Why do I need the luck?"

"From what I've heard about Sammi, she goes through men pretty quickly. Doesn't stick with one for very long."

"Ah. You worry about my delicate heart." The other man chuckles.

"I've been seeing her sister. Tango," Joe finally admits.

"A sister? It is hard to imagine two such beautiful women in the same family."

"They don't look that much alike."

"So you are dating the...ugly sister?" Even I can tell by Nicky's tone that he is teasing Joe.

Still, Joe takes the bait. "She isn't ugly. She's...interesting. Different."

I was hoping for cute.

"I have heard of this. You are saying she has good personality."

Joe laughs. "She does, but that's not what I'm saying. There's something about her. Something..."

"Ah. You find her intriguing," Nicky puts in helpfully.

"Yes. Intriguing. But also frustrating. She's as hard to pin down as Sammi apparently is."

"Oh?"

I hear shifting as if positions are being changed. The tinkle of ice in a glass.

"Go ahead. Try mixing business with pleasure with Sammi. Just don't say I didn't warn you," Joe says in a tone that sounds like he is only half-joking.

"Perhaps we should have a date together. If we join forces, we may be able to pin them down as you say." Now it's his companion's turn to use that half-joking tone.

"We can try it, Nicky. But don't be surprised if Tee shows up with another man even though she has a date with me."

Nicky bursts out laughing. I burn with humiliation to hear Joe discussing my behavior so casually with another man. One time that happened. *One time*! Yet he's acting like I two-time him on a regular basis.

But more importantly, I concentrate on the name Nicky. The accent. The upscale home. Could this possibly be the man Lenny discovered who had a connection to the Albanians? How can I find out if Joe's friend Nicky and Nickolai Stakosha are, as I suspect, one and the same?

I hear the murmur of their voices but I stop listening to the words. I need to figure out exactly where I am. I head through the landscaping toward the front of the house. If I follow the driveway to the road, keeping carefully to the side, of course, even from my limited viewing area so close to the ground, I might find a landmark of some kind to tell me where this house is. I disturb a cricket along the way and somehow manage to capture him and eat him. I'm not aware of any specific taste, merely a squirming and a bit of crunching before he disappears.

Before I reach the driveway, I know exactly how to discover Nicky's identity. If Joe suggests a double date with a friend of his, I'll agree. I'll encourage Sammi to accept such an invitation. If I could I'd do a fist pump to punctuate my progress in infiltrating the Espresso Mafia's operation.

Sasha, I am sure, will be impressed.

Chapter Twenty-one

May you be protected with strong bolts, Of iron and bronze,

As Sasha instructed, I drove around and took random streets to get to the mall. In the parking lot I cruised up and down the rows, parking once and idling, always checking for a tail. I honestly don't think anyone followed me but I'm not an expert yet at spotting them if they did. I park near the theater and meander on foot, zigzagging and backtracking several times, just to be sure. I don't see anything suspicious. I wait until a couple of other shoppers head toward the east entrance and position myself a couple of steps behind them.

I burst through the east entrance of Gulf Coast Mall feeling higher than a kite. Adrenaline buzzes through my system as I keep to the same pattern inside, entering random stores, walking up one aisle and down another, keeping an eye out for anyone suspicious who appears to be interested in my movements. Again, I see no one. Steadily I work my way toward Sears where I take a circuitous route to the exit on the west side of the mall.

Once I'm in the parking lot I walk up and down the rows of parked cars. Sasha will find me.

He does, pulling up in his gray sedan. I slide into the passenger seat, and notice that the overhead light does not come on. It is just past eight-thirty in the evening. By the time we arrive at the location of the warehouse it will be full dark.

I can almost reach out and touch the tension radiating off Sasha. I have an adrenaline buzz but he is wired. I study him in the light allowed by other cars and streetlights as we head out of town. He is dressed in black. So am I. "I wasn't followed," I say.

"Are you sure?"

"As sure as I can be. I did everything you told me to do."

"They are experts."

"I'm not an idiot." I sound like a sulky teenager, a trait which Sasha seems to bring out in me. Maybe he deserves it since he wasn't around to experience my sulkiness during my teens.

Sasha runs a hand through his hair and glances in the rearview mirror before he turns. He sighs and maybe a little of the tension leaves with the expulsion of air. "I do not mean to insult you."

He doesn't look at me when he says it. He is concentrating on his driving and the constant checks in rearview and side mirrors. But his expression changes subtly.

"I know you don't." I stare ahead wishing there was some way to make the awkwardness between us go away.

"I am not good...saying things."

After a pause and another sigh he speaks again. "I am used to working alone. I do not worry."

"You don't have to worry about me."

"I must. These are dangerous people."

"I'm aware."

Again the hand through the hair. "You do not know." He sounds sad and resigned.

"I'd pursue them with or without you, so you shouldn't feel responsible. If you weren't around, you wouldn't even know I was doing it."

"I want you only to be safe."

"Sasha, no one's safe. Ever. We think we are. We live with that illusion. But the truth is none of us are. Danger and tragedy can be around a corner and we never see it coming. If you want to take me back to my car we can call it quits right now. I'll keep after these guys until I get to the bottom of whatever they're doing. I'll expose them, have them arrested and put in jail for life if that's what it takes. I want us to work together, but if you don't want to I'll do it without you."

Sasha glances away from the road for a moment and I see a glimmer of a smile playing around his lips. At least I think it might be a smile. I know I've won. He needs me. Almost as much as I need him.

"This is the street?" he asks thirty minutes later. He slows and we cruise on past. "It is a dead end."

"All these streets run perpendicular to canals."

"How far is the house?" He slows and makes a U-turn since there is no traffic from either direction.

"If I had to guess, I'd say a half mile, maybe."

We pass the street. Sasha peers at it, but beyond the streetlight at the corner all is darkness. He turns down the next street and drives slowly. There are mailboxes placed at random intervals along either side of the road. A few lights show from the houses set at the ends of driveways beyond the trees.

"Do you know approximately where on the street the warehouse sits?" Sasha glanced from one side of the road to the other as he drove.

"At the end."

"Perfect." He turns off the car's headlights and rolls to a stop on a small apron at the end of the street. He turns off the ignition. "If we follow the canal we should come upon it from the rear, correct?"

"Yes, but..."

There is enough light coming from the dashboard to allow me to see Sasha's eyebrow raise.

"It's dark. There could be alligators, or—or snakes." I can't help the shiver that runs up my spine. The memory of my encounter with the snake, *as a snake*, gives me the heebie jeebies.

"If you are afraid, you may stay here."

There is that glint of something in his eyes again, that brief moment when he almost might smile.

"I didn't say I was afraid."

We get out of the car. I'd planned ahead and taken the tiny flashlight with the super powerful beam off my key ring and put it in my pocket. I also had my gun tucked into the back waistband of my pants. If a snake or an alligator posed a problem I'd shoot first and ask questions later. I put on the black ball cap I'd brought. I'm ready to go.

"Let's not use flashlights unless we need them," Sasha says softly. He starts off toward the canal. I follow although I don't see how we won't need flashlights. There isn't much moonlight and there are a lot of clouds.

My night vision adjusted and with the water reflecting what little light there is, it's easier to navigate than I thought it would be. The canals that make up the drainage system in the outlying areas of Silvergate aren't deep, I'd guess surely no more than six or eight feet even during the height of the summer rainy season.

There are rustlings here and there, probably small creatures disturbed by our trespass. There are a few night noises from insects and frogs but other than the noise Sasha and I make as we walk, it is fairly quiet.

I wish I'd brought bug spray. Mosquitoes whine close to my ears. I slap at them subtly. They don't seem to be bother Sasha at all or if they are he ignores them. I trudge along behind him. This close to the canal the undergrowth is easier to navigate.

When he stops suddenly I almost run into him. "You didn't tell me there was a fence."

I stare at the barely visible chain link fence. "I forgot."

"We go around."

"Not up and over?"

"Not yet."

I think maybe he is smiling.

I stay behind him as we follow the fence across the back of the property and along the side until we are at the front corner. Away from the canal, the darkness is an almost overwhelming, pitch black. Without the fence to guide me, I'd be walking blind. The urge to turn on my flashlight just for a moment is strong but I resist. I'll prove to Sasha that I'm just as tough as he is or die trying.

Sasha is still, listening, sensing or planning. I have no idea what he's doing.

"There is a gate?" he queries softly.

"Yes. Chained and padlocked. There's a gravel driveway."

"Security lights? Alarm system?"

"I don't know. I don't think there are security lights. If there's an alarm system it's silent."

We wait in silence for another few minutes before he touches my arm and start moving. We step down the slope of the swale and jump across its muddy depth, not an easy feat in the dark. It's amazing how other senses come into play when one is lost. It's easy to know by the squish of the mud and the way my shoes react to the soggier ground, where the water begins. I have a good idea how far it is to the other side and that the incline of the slope is similar.

We keep to the far side of the road and creep slowly past the warehouse. I can see the outline, or think I can, of the fence and the lighter shade of the gravel driveway. Sasha does not linger. Once we reach the end of the road where it dead ends at the canal, we cross back over and begin following the canal back to our starting point.

Reconnoitering, I think with a smile. This is a part of the spying process, I suppose. There is probably a lot of watching and waiting. Boring work where nothing at all happens. I'm not sure I have the patience for it.

I am happy to be in Sasha's company and beyond pleased that we are working together. I can only hope there will be more nights like this in our future.

I trudge along behind Sasha through the lot behind the warehouse. Up ahead I can make out the glint of Sasha's car through the tangled bushes and weeds. Sasha stops just before a gloved hand clamps me in a choke hold and the muzzle of a gun presses against my temple. My backside is pressed up against a hard male body.

I don't dare move even if the shock of being accosted hadn't frozen me. I can see the glint of a gun held to Sasha's head by what looks like an alien being, but is evidently another man dressed in black. His face is obscured by what I decide are night-vision goggles and he wears a black baseball cap.

"Want to explain what you're doing here?" he asks Sasha. His voice is a low, gravelly growl.

"I'm happy to," Sasha replies. "If you'd like to lower your weapon. I am unarmed."

"She's not," says the guy holding me. He takes his hand away from my mouth and fumbles at my waistband. He holds my gun by the barrel pointing it down.

"It's registered," is all I can think to say.

That earns both of us a pat-down. Mine isn't extremely thorough or intimate, which makes me wonder who these guys are. If they are of the criminal element they are being awfully nice to us when they have no reason to be.

Sasha's keeper repeats his demand for an explanation of our presence. Sasha says something to him I don't catch, and they step away closer to the car. I can hear them murmuring to each other but I can't make out the words.

My guy stays close to me. My night vision has improved quite a bit. A few stars make an appearance which helps. I can see the outline of him, but that is about it. I get the impression he is younger than his companion, which I base on his voice and the way he handles himself.

"We come in peace," I venture. I give him the Vulcan fingers-separated gesture.

To my surprise he chuckles. "We already ran your plates."

"Then what was that surprise attack about?"

I think I see him give a little shrug. "Better safe than sorry."

"Can I have my gun back?"

He glances in the direction of the other two. "In a bit."

"Who are you guys?"

"ATF."

I am not only surprised he answers me, but at his answer. ATF agents. Which means what? That what I think is in that warehouse might actually be accurate. Not alcohol. Not tobacco. Firearms. So I'm not the only one aware of the Mafia's suspicious activities in this remote location.

"What are you doing out here?"

As far as I know, Sasha and I haven't done anything wrong. We haven't broken any laws, except maybe trespassing on private property. But it is highly unlikely the owners of said property will press charges even if they knew we trespassed. I don't have to tell this guy anything.

I stare at him although I can't tell if he's staring back at me through his night vision goggles or not. Probably he is.

"You're pretty cute," he says.

"I am not."

"Yeah. You are. Maybe we can—"

"Chip," his partner hisses through the darkness. "Let's go."

Chip touches my elbow and indicates for me to precede him. Sasha is waiting at the car. The two agents start walking down the road.

"Hey," I call, not trying to keep my voice down. "My gun."

Chip halts and comes back to me with the gun held out butt first. "See you around," he says. I see his smile.

"Yeah, right."

I shove the gun back into my waistband and get into the car. We pass the two agents and then their black SUV parked on the shoulder. We continue on in silence. Sasha turns onto the crossroad and accelerates before he says, "You should not have a gun."

"You have one."

"Yes, but." He shoves his hand through his hair.

"But what? I don't have the right to defend myself?"

"Of course you do."

"Then what's the problem?"

"My daughter should not have reason to defend herself."

I look out my window. A short time ago I had no such need. Not only had I been virtually invisible to the rest of the world, I'd also been powerless. Swallowing that first forbidden bean changed everything. It couldn't be undone.

Chapter Twenty-two

You have never before been where we are going now

Normally, I avoid valet parking, although it's not like I go to a lot of places where it's an option. But I am not going to hike up the sloped driveway from all the way across the Heritage Bay Country Club parking lot tonight. Not when I'm dressed to the nines and have taken a lot of extra time with makeup. My smoky eyes were not going to perspire into raccoon eyes before I even reach the foyer.

I hand Monty's ignition key to the valet and tuck the ticket into my beaded evening bag. Another white-liveried attendant sweeps open one of a pair of eight-foot glass-paned doors for me and I step inside.

No expense was spared in the design of the Heritage Bay Country Club. Creamy marble tile stretches across the floor. A multi-tiered chandelier with ropes of beading sends spears of light across the space. Small seating areas are grouped here and there, filled with clubby cushioned chairs and sturdy yet elegant tables and lamps. A dramatic fireplace commands attention with its inviting gas flames.

A few other guests are gathered here and there, greeting each other and chatting, but the echoes of the party itself come from a mezzanine level reached by a wide marble staircase to the left.

In my strappy heels, I pick my way across the slippery marble. I gain confidence by the time I've climbed the stairs where the marble ends and something more durable, travertine perhaps, prevails.

The party has that early, echoey sound, as pockets of guests vie for drinks at the bar, slap each other on the back and peruse the buffet tables filled with finger foods.

I pause at the side of the stairs, straining to see Joe. He'd regretted not picking me up, but he had to be here much earlier to oversee the arrangements.

While I searched the crowd, other arriving guests pass by me. One of them surprised me by saying, "Hello, Tee."

Lenny squeezes my elbow and moves in, pressing his cheek to mine in greeting. "I love that dress," he whispers before he straightens. It is the same dress I'd worn to his father's birthday party a few weeks ago. The only little black dress I own, in fact.

I stare at Lenny. Frankly, I can't help it. I haven't seen him in a few days, and even though he is still recognizable as Lenny, he'd changed a few things about his appearance. For one, he'd cut his hair. Gone were the multi-colored streaks and spikes and layers. Actually, some of the longish layers are still there, but his hair is one color, sort of a medium brown, or maybe a dark blond. His clothes fit fairly well, but Lenny is never going to be a conformist. He has on a tuxedo jacket and a white button-down shirt, over a pair of dark blue jeans and black loafers worn without socks. Dangling in the shirt's vee, in lieu of a tie perhaps, is a strip of leather knotted around some dull stones.

I feel that odd little tug of interest that hits me whenever I'm around Lenny. Like there is more to him than meets the eye. I squelch it down, however, like I always do, and remind myself Lenny is a friend, nothing more. I am, after all, crazy about Joe.

"I didn't know you'd be here," I say to Lenny when I finally get done checking him out.

"There are a lot of things you don't know about me, Tee," he says with a smile.

He'd read my mind. Freaky.

"Scott!" Someone calls from behind him.

We both turn to see his parents, Shelly and Steve Schutzel reaching the top of the stairs. His mother looks fabulous for a woman her age. I wonder how much botox and cosmetic surgery she partakes of on an annual basis. The work she's had done is all very subtle, of course, as only the fabulously wealthy can do it. Nails, dress, hair, jewelry. Tasteful and expensive. That's what Shelly Schutzel's appearance projects.

Like most of the other male guests, Dr. Schutzel wears a suit and a tie, managing to look both sophisticated and relaxed. They greet me and we move as a group into the crowd. In seconds a server approaches to take our drink orders. I don't want to walk around with a beer bottle in my hand and I know I can sip vodka and cranberry slowly. I will not do anything to embarrass Joe on his big night.

Distracted by small talk with Lenny and his parents, I temporarily forget to look for Joe. He, however, spots me and slides effortlessly into our group by slipping an arm around my waist and kissing my temple. "There's my girl." The ripple that goes through me when Joe touches me is completely different from the spark of interest Lenny ignites.

Joe greets Lenny and the two shake hands. Lenny introduces Joe to his parents. More handshaking and small talk ensue. Our drinks arrive. Friends of the Schutzel's pull them away and Joe excuses us from Lenny as well. He links his fingers through mine and leads me through the growing crowd.

While before there was subtle background music playing, I see now there is a three-piece band throwing themselves into full-throttle entertainment mode by increasing the volume and tempo of the songs. Conversation becomes louder as more bodies press into the party and voices raise to be heard.

I see a man who looks like my father across the room, but Joe and I are weaving our way through the crowd and there is too much movement. The man was dressed in a suit and tie with his hair slicked back, and he wore wire-rimmed glasses. I tell myself it can't be Sasha, that he wouldn't be here. Unless he is doing the same thing I'm doing. In spite of his disguise I am certain I recognized him. I try to see where he might have gone, but it is hopeless. What was I going to do anyway? Introduce him to everyone as my father?

"There's your sister," Joe informs me, just as I spot Sammi's blond head and plunging neckline. Next to her is a tall, darkly handsome man with close-cropped hair and vaguely foreign features. He smiles and I see his teeth are white though slightly crooked which doesn't detract from his overall appeal.

"Tee, you look darling!" Sammi greets me. Her hug buries me in a cloud of Angel perfume and cleavage. Her green halter dress clings and plunges in all the right places, setting her assets off to perfection.

"Meet Nicky," she enthuses when she straightens, indicating Mr. Tall, Dark and Handsome.

"Nickolai Strakosha, at your service, madamoiselle," he says with a glint of humor in his dark eyes. He lifts my hand and brushes my knuckles with a kiss. Something shivers inside me.

"Ignore him," Sammi suggests. "He's being ridiculously Romanian tonight."

"Always," he returns with a grin at Sammi and what I take for a sharp perusal of me. "Not just tonight. How can I not be ridiculously dazzled when in the company of two such beautiful women?"

That answered that question. The Nicky whom I'd overheard talking to Joe while I spent time in the body of a turtle and Nickolai Strakosha were one and the same. And Nickolai Strakosha had ties to the Albanians. Which means both my boyfriend and my sister are friendly with the possible head of a criminal organization.

I nibble the inside of my lip while I think about what, if anything, my next step should be.

"Excuse me. I'll be right back," Joe says.

I glance around to see Dan Whiting, the club manager, signaling to Joe. At the same time I see Lenny chatting with a small group of guests. He happens to glance my way. I raise my eyebrows in Nicky's direction hoping Lenny will get the message and join us. Before I tune back in to what Sammi is saying I see him excuse himself and head my way.

"Tee." He nods at me when he wedges in between me and Sammi.

"Lenny! Hi!" I act like I hadn't seen him a few minutes ago. "Meet my sister Sammi and Nicky, was it? Strakosha?" Academy Award time for me.

"Nice to meet you both." As usual, Lenny's manners are impeccable. He smiles at Sammi and shakes Nicky's hand.

"Looks like Heritage Bay is going to be quite a success," he comments, glancing around at the animated crowd.

"It's definitely the hottest property at the moment," Sammi agrees giving Lenny a speculative look. "Have you seen the models?"

"Forgive her," I say to Lenny. "Sammi's a local real estate mogul and she's always trolling for new clients."

Sammi laughs. "It is what I do."

"Darling," Nicky drawls. "You do not need him. You have me."

"Right," Sammi returns. "As if I could ever pin you down and make a sale."

"Ah. On the contrary. I look forward to being pinned down by you."

There is a hum of sexual chemistry between them that goes beyond their banter. Ugh, is all I can think after witnessing Sammi's behavior with Marco. I do not want the mental image of Nickolai Strakosha in bed with my sister. Which reminds me uncomfortably of Dr. Parker and her relationship with Sammi.

"Would you excuse us?" Lenny asks Nicky and Sammi. "There's someone I'd like Tee to meet."

I allow Lenny to draw me away from the two of them. Truth be told I can't help but sense Nick Strakosha's questioning gaze on me when he thinks no one else will notice. I've completely lost track of Joe. This party isn't turning out exactly the way I'd expected.

Lenny pauses at the perimeter of the crowd and gazes at me for a moment. "Very casually," he says. "Turn your head to your right like you're scanning the crowd looking for someone."

I do and I know immediately who it is he wants me to see. I allow my gaze to pass over Tirana as if I'd barely noticed her at all and return my attention to Lenny.

"See her?"

"Yes."

"She's one. There's at least one more, possibly two."

"You've been busy." I smile like we're small talking and take a sip of my drink. The ice had melted and watered it down, but I don't care. A server stops next to us to offer bacon-wrapped scallops or miniature spring rolls. We decline and he moves on.

"I don't have a date, so I have a lot of free time."

That is a blatant dig at me, because if I gave Lenny one iota of encouragement we both knew he'd be all over me. I feel certain, however, that if Lenny wanted to have a date this evening he wouldn't have had any problem finding a willing female. The lovely Lily perhaps.

"I don't seem to have a date, either," I inform him. Joe has virtually abandoned me.

"Look," Lenny hisses, gazing over my shoulder intently.

I turn casually, just in time to see Tirana disappear down the marble steps. A dapper gentlemen who has to be in his sixties, gives a furtive glance around before following her.

"Where are they going?" I whisper. I turn to stand next to Lenny so I can see without turning around.

"My guess would be the men's locker room," he replies tersely.

While we watch another young woman in a server's uniform heads down the stairs. A few seconds behind her another male guest follows. He doesn't bother to see if anyone notices his departure.

"Want to check it out?" Lenny asks.

I look around the crowded room. The party is in full swing. I still haven't spotted Joe. I have nothing better to do. "Sure. Why not?"

I set my glass on one of the tables and we weave around the edge of the crowd to the stairs. I hold on to the banister and Lenny takes my hand to help me down the slippery steps. At the bottom, he lets go.

At the rear of the foyer there is an elaborately diagrammed floorplan of the clubhouse but Lenny ignores it. He evidently already knows his way around.

Three broad hallways branch off the foyer. According to the directional arrows and signage to the right is the restaurant. Straight ahead are the women's locker room and lounge. On the left lay the men's locker room and lounge area and straight ahead is the pro shop and the exit to the cart barn.

The hallways are carpeted which hushes our footsteps. Lenny slows, pretending I suppose, to be merely having a look around and not looking for anything or anyone in particular.

There are closed doors along the way labeled with their purpose. Massage. Exercise. Card Room. Supplies. Outside the mens' locker room Lenny eases one of the doors open an inch at a time until we can see inside. I get a glimpse of a more durable carpet in forest green and lots of white subway tile on the walls. On one side of a short hallway is a sauna. On the other a steam room.

"Stay here," Lenny whispers. He pushes the door open and slides inside. The solid wood panel whooshes softly behind him. I debate for about thirty seconds about whether to ignore his instructions. His presence in a mens' locker room won't be questioned whereas mine might if I follow him in. A tour of the entire club isn't on the agenda for the party-goers as far as I know, unless of course, they are serious contenders for membership. Even then, I expect they'd arrange a tour with the club's sales department. Still, Lenny might be forgiven for taking his own private unguided and unauthorized tour.

At the end of my debate I decide to simply wait for him. I trust Lenny. He won't do anything stupid and he'll bring me back a full report. That's what I'm thinking when I sense a presence behind me. I turn just in time to catch a whiff of tobacco and onion-scented breath along with a glimpse of a meaty fist head my way.

Chapter Twenty-three

Crush those who are their enemies,

My cheek is pressed against a hard flat surface. I have a monster headache. Plus I'm damp, perspiring and decidedly uncomfortable. I lift my head tentatively. Pain explodes from the base of my skull and radiates upward. I groan and try to orient myself while slowly pushing myself into a sitting position. Sweat rolls off my face. My hair is wet with it and so are my clothes. Everything is damp and uncomfortable, including the tile floor. The heat is almost unbearable. Mists of steamy vapor nearly obscure my vision but I can make out white-tiled walls and two levels of tiered bench seating.

I twist around without turning my head and can just make out another body, fully-clothed like me, damp and crumpled, but with one significant difference. A pool of blood has gathered near the head of the body.

Lenny! my aching brain screams silently.

I half slide-half crawl across the floor to him and squeeze his bicep. "Lenny," I hiss. I shake him a little. "Lenny! Wake up." He groans. Panicked I turn around, searching for a door. I know exactly where we are. In the steam room next to the men's locker room. The big display at the entrance to the club touted all the amenities a man could want. Although, frankly, I'd never understood what a steam room did for anyone. I'd grown up in Florida. If you wanted to sweat in a steamy environment, all you had to do was walk out your front door in the middle of July and voila! Instant steam bath.

There has to be a door, but I wonder if I'll be able to find it the way the steam is obscuring my vision. I look back at Lenny. His arm moves beneath my hand and he struggles to a sitting position. I stare at the misty dark pool where his head had been.

I shove my face close to his. "Are you okay? You're bleeding."

Lenny can't quite focus on me and it takes him a few seconds to answer. He reaches to the back of his head and his fingers come away streaked with blood. We stare at each other for another few seconds. "We've got to get out of here," I inform him unnecessarily. "Or we're going to melt."

Lenny's blood-streaked fingers are pruny-looking already. I imagine mine are the same. "Let's find the door." I stand unsteadily on the slippery tile. I step out of my pretty strappy sandals. I'm not going to impress anyone with my fashion sense for the rest of the evening. I step next to the raised seating area and keep my hand on it to guide me. Quickly, I reach the end of it, follow the right angle and find the door. I feel for a handle and push it down. It doesn't budge. I push it up. It doesn't budge. I do both with more force. There is no give at all. I bend to examine the handle. There is no lock that I can see. Which means the door is otherwise blocked.

Lenny has followed me and he nudges me aside to try the handle for himself. His superior male strength is no match for the handle. With both fists I pound on the door and start yelling at the top of my lungs. Lenny joins me. Nothing happens. No one comes. No one hears us. Why would they? We are far from the reception rooms where there is the noise of a hundred conversations and live music.

We exhaust ourselves in less than a minute. Lenny slumps down hard on the bench. He leans over and puts his head in his hands. I fumble my way back across the floor to discover my shoes and my evening bag nearby. I fish for my cell phone before I remember I didn't bring it. "I don't have my cell phone." I say. "Do you have yours?"

Lenny pats his pants pockets then feels inside first one then the other. "No. I left it in the car." I don't like the way his voice sounds, like he is fading away or something.

Where is Joe? Hasn't he come looking for me?

Of course he has, I chastise myself. He'll assume I'm somewhere in the crowd of guests just as he is. The first place he looks will not be the men's locker room area.

"How you doing, Lenny?"

His voice, disembodied through the vapor-laden air, replies, "Not so good."

That isn't the answer I hoped for. I need to keep Lenny moving, keep him thinking, so he can help get us out of here. "Is there a window in that door, do you remember?"

I don't have my cell phone but my gun is in the zipper compartment of my purse. Not loaded, of course. I kept the three-step rule in mind. I'm not even sure why I brought my gun except I like carrying it. It makes me feel powerful and ridiculously special. I allow myself some grim satisfaction that our assailants didn't discover the gun. They probably hadn't searched my purse. How many women carried a gun in their evening bag? Not many, I suppose, which is why the thugs never thought to search for one in mine.

I hear the muffled movements of Lenny rising and examining the door. "There's a small window, here," he says. I hear him rap his knuckles against it.

The zipper compartment of my purse also contains one clip of ammo. I hold the gun and the clip close to my face, mentally review the procedure for loading it, and then follow it. I am locked and loaded.

"What are you doing?"

"I've got a gun," I inform him. "And I'm not afraid to use it to get us out of here."

"What are you going to do?" He sounds dubiously suspicious, a bit too much like Cody.

"I might be able to shoot out the window, don't you think? At least we can get some air. Then we can call for help. Or figure out why the door won't open."

"A bullet might not penetrate the window. If it's tempered glass, which it probably is."

"Do you have a better idea?" I challenge him. "We're already dehydrated. How much longer do you think we're going to last? For that matter, doesn't a steam room have an automatic shut-off valve or something? It's just getting hotter and hotter in here."

"Maybe whoever shoved us in here deactivated it."

"Trying to break the window is our best shot at getting out of here. No pun intended." I shuffle in the direction of Lenny's voice until I come up against him. "Where's the window?"

He takes my hand and slides it up along the slick metal of the door. "Right here." With his hand covering mine, he runs my palm around the perimeter of the window and then along the glass. I guess it to be about a foot square or a little less and about five feet from the floor.

"How are you going to see it to shoot at it?" Lenny coughs. He begins to wheeze.

"I'm not going to be able to," I acknowledge. The steam seems to feed upon itself. My hands are slick with moisture. I wonder if I'll be able to hang on to the gun to take a shot.

I'll be shooting blind at a relatively small target. If I miss the window the bullet might ricochet off the metal door and God only knew what might happen then. It might boomerang right back at me. But right now it seems like this is our only chance.

I make a decision. I raise my arms and hold the gun with both hands so it's level with the middle of the window. "Here's what we're going to do. I'm going to walk straight back a couple of feet just like this and take a shot. Maybe two."

"I'm going to duck," Lenny wheezes.

"Exactly. I want you down, flat on the floor, probably along this first tier, okay?"

"Okay."

"Let's do it."

I walk backward four steps. Already my arms feel unsteady and the gun slippery in my hands. No guts no glory, I remind myself. "Ready?" I ask Lenny.

"Ready," comes his muffled reply.

I close my eyes and squeeze the trigger. The noise sounds deafening in the small space. I think I hear something shatter. I chance one more shot before my arms give out. I lower them. Definitely I heard glass tinkling against tile and sense a rush of non-steam-laden air.

"I think you did it," Lenny rasps. He hauls himself to his feet as I approach the door.

Definitely, the window is broken. "Can you clear away those jagged edges?" I ask him.

Lenny covers his hand with his coat sleeve and shoves against the shards of glass until they fall outside the door.

"Want to lift me up? Maybe I can reach the handle and get the door open from the outside."

"I'll try."

Poor Lenny. He always seems to get the short end of the deal when he helps me.

"Use my jacket to cover the bottom of the window so you don't get scraped up."

He grasps me around the hips and hoists me up. I stick my head through the window and looked down to discover a golf club wedged under the door handle. It is a perfect fit for the space between the handle and the floor. No wonder we couldn't budge it. I shift back enough to get my left arm and shoulder through the window opening. "I think I can reach it," I inform Lenny. Push me up a little more."

He complies by using both hands on my rear end and giving me a little push. I stretch and strain and reach. My fingertips brush the top of the club. I grunt and stretch as much as I can, pushing myself against the small opening until I can push the club a little away from the door.

"Try the handle," I shout to Lenny. "We've almost got it." I shove against the handle from the outside at the same time Lenny pushes against it from the inside. The golf club wobbles and falls. The door bursts open just as I hear someone shout my name and a thunder of footsteps heading our way.

Lenny collapses through the door while still holding on to the lower half of my body accidentally yanking me down on top of him. The air leaves his lungs in a whoosh and the door bangs back against both of us.

The outer doors bang open and Joe skids to a halt. "Tee, my God!" "What happened? Are you alright?"

I crawl off of Lenny, too shaken to answer Joe just then.

"Lenny?" Steam continues to pour out into the corridor. I have the sense of other people crowding in behind Joe, gathering around us, and multiple voices raised in confusion. I look past him and see my father. He shoves a hand through his slicked-back hair and gives me a look I can't decipher before he melts back into the crowd.

"Call nine-one-one," Joe tells someone in a terse tone.

He crouches next to me. "Lenny?" I say again. I brush my fingers against Lenny's wet hair. We are both a mess. Bedraggled doesn't begin to describe what we must look like.

"Find that damn shut-off valve and turn off the heat." That's Joe again, issuing an order to someone in the group surrounding us.

"Lenny!" I am near tears. If Lenny dies because of me, because I got him involved in pursuing the Espresso Mafia, I will never forgive myself. I lay my head against his chest. His heart is beating. Thank God.

"Let me through, let me through," comes another voice behind the crowd. "I'm a doctor." It's Lenny's dad.

Joe helps me up just as Steve wedges his way through the other onlookers. He glances at me. "Are you okay, Tee?"

"Yes."

He drops to his knees next to his son and lifts Lenny's wrist. "Scott? Can you hear me?"

"He was bleeding before. Someone hit him on the back of the head," I inform Dr. Schutzel.

Lenny's eyes flutter open. His gaze skips past his father to Joe then locks on me. I think he shakes his head slightly in some sort of silent communication. I nod imperceptibly. I know what he is saying. We don't know anything. We were merely curious about the rest of the country club and decided to explore a bit. We were assaulted and left in the steam room. There will be no mention of following Tirana, or the Espresso Mafia.

Chapter Twenty-four

And preserve him from every harm

"I'm sorry I ruined your party." It is hours later and Joe is driving me home. I toy with the edge of the third towel I'd been wrapped in since I escaped the steam room. My dress is ruined as are my shoes probably and my little beaded purse. Water and heat do not pair well with silk, velvet and leather.

Joe has been frighteningly silent ever since I fell out of the steam room on top of Lenny. Since I've been bracing myself for Joe to dump me almost from the first moment I saw him, I figure tonight is the night. I ruined what was probably the biggest night of his career. I did it quite publicly and stunningly with another man at my side. I can only imagine what kind of horrible publicity the Seagate Sentinel will generate once they got hold of the statement I gave to the police.

Lenny revived fairly quickly once he rehydrated, but his father insisted on at least an overnight stay in the hospital. He refused to take any chances after he examined Lenny's head injury.

I'd also been checked over by the paramedics, ironically the same ones who'd shown up after I'd been assaulted inside my own apartment by a member of the Espresso Mafia disguised as a flower delivery man. I had a nice lump on the back of my head, and they'd removed some bits of glass from the soles of my feet, but that was it. I drank water until I was sure all my bodily fluids had been replaced. Other than the dull throb from the head wound, I feel all right.

I glance out the window and blink rapidly when Joe makes no reply to my apology. I will probably never see him again which is exactly what I deserve. I am still amazed that he ever showed any interest in me in the first place. Trouble is I really, really, really like him. I close my eyes for a second and relive every one of his kisses. No guy had ever kissed me the way Joe had. Or at least, I never had that same warm melty sensation I get when Joe kisses me. That's all we've done so far. Kissed. But I am hooked. If he kisses me tonight, he'll be kissing me goodbye.

At my apartment complex he parks and kills the engine, gets out and comes around to open my door. Always the gentleman. Without a word he guides me up the stairs with his hand on the small of my back. I can feel the tension running through him. I can't tell if it is caused by anger held in check. I've never known Joe to be so closed and silent. But maybe I just never gave him a reason to behave this way in my company.

I find my keys in my still damp purse and unlock my door. I start to tell him he doesn't have to come in, that he doesn't have to explain, but he propels me inside the apartment and comes in behind me.

I turn toward him. "Joe, you—"

His arms wrap around me and he holds me tightly against the length of his body. "Dammit, Tee, you scare the hell out of me."

I am shocked into silence. Now is probably not a good time to tell him I scare the hell out of myself as well.

"I looked all over that damn party for you and when I couldn't find you I don't know why but I got this weird feeling that something was wrong, that something had happened to you." Joe shudders. "Then I heard those gunshots, and I thought..."

He sucks in a breath. I can feel him shaking his head back and forth above mine. My face is pressed into his shoulder and frankly it is the loveliest feeling. I can smell the starch from his shirt as well as a trace of his cologne. But beneath all that is the man scent of Joe himself. I slide my arms around his waist and hug him hard. What he seems to be saying is that he was worried about me.

He shifts back a little and cradles my head in both his hands. He looks into my eyes like he's searching for something. "If anything happened to you..." He brushes his fingers through my hair as if contemplating the possibility.

He kisses me hungrily. I kiss him back. This sure doesn't feel like a goodbye kiss. This feels like a let's-move-this-to-the-bedroom kiss.

When it ends, without us moving one step closer to the bedroom, Joe rests his forehead against mine still holding my head in his hands. "I want to know what's going on," he says softly.

"What's going on?" I echo. "Do you mean about—about—what?"

Joe smiles. "About you. What are you into? Who's after you?"

I can't speak. Certainly can't answer such a question. I've been warned, for one thing. Whether they are misinformed about who my "boyfriend" is or not, I'm not taking any chances with Joe's safety. Lenny has already been injured twice. Cody once, although in truth, that had nothing to do with his connection to me. Whether or not my actions while in the body of a spider damaged his career remain to be seen. The less Joe knows the better.

When I don't immediately answer him, Joe lifts his head. He drops his hands and steps back. We are less than a foot apart but the distance between us is much greater. How can I explain anything to Joe even if I want to? My transformations? My suspicions about the Albanians? The encounters with my father.

I'll lose him for sure if I tell him the truth, even a portion of it. The less he knows the better, for his own sake as well as my peace of mind. "I can't tell you."

"Can't or won't?"

"Can't. I can tell you I'm not involved in anything illegal." *Not yet anyway.*

That gets half of a disbelieving laugh out of him. He waits for me to say something else.

"Do you want some coffee?"

He lifts a hand and lets it drop. "Sure. I guess."

What I want is to get out my ruined still-damp clothes. I dash into the kitchen and put coffee on in what is record time even for me. "Make yourself comfortable." I wave a hand in the direction of the living room as I speed through on my way to my bedroom.

I strip off my dress and underwear and pull on a tee shirt and drawstring shorts. When I reappear in the living room I see Joe took me at my word. The television is on ESPN with the volume so low I can't hear it. His shoes are side-by-side near the end table. He tossed his jacket and tie across the back of a chair. His cuffs are rolled up and the top two buttons of his shirt are undone. He is sprawled on my sofa and I think he looks sexy as hell. He gives me a sleepy look.

"Do you still want coffee?"

"I think I'm going to need it."

He follows me into the kitchen and watches me get mugs out of the cabinet and pour coffee. I hand one to him. "Sugar, right?" I set the bowl next to him on the counter.

He gives me a sleepy, sexy smile. "You know me so well."

"Do I?"

"I bet you know what I'm thinking right now." His stomach growls.

I chuckle. "You want something to eat?"

"What have you got?"

I open the refrigerator and peer inside. Joe comes up behind me and looks over my shoulder. "Eggs. Cheese. Lettuce."

"Bread?"

"I have bread. Egg sandwich?"

"Sounds good. One thing I do know how to make is toast."

We make our sandwiches and take them and our coffee to the table. There is an odd kind of intimacy between us now. The wee hours of the morning, sharing a simple meal in a dimly lit apartment. "So what can you tell me?" Joe asks when we are nearly finished eating.

"Nothing."

"How about if I ask you questions and you give me yes or no answers?"

"I'd rather you didn't."

"Are you working undercover?"

Now it is my turn for the disbelieving half-laugh. I might be unrecognizable at times, but I can answer Joe truthfully. "No."

"Are you a cop?"

At least Joe is asking easy questions even if I don't want to play along. "No."

"Do you work for the government?"

I grin at the very idea. "No."

"A government other than ours?"

"Joe. Come on."

"Are you a spy?"

I can only think of one thing to make him stop asking me questions. I get up from my chair and move toward his. I bend down and kiss him. "Yes." He pushes his chair back from the table. I crawl into his lap. "I'm a spy." Between kisses I keep talking. "I know all sorts of things I shouldn't." *True*. "All sorts of things I wish I didn't know." *True*.

"What about Lenny?"

Is Joe purposely trying to kill the mood? He isn't hiding evidence of his interest in me, but he won't shut up, either. I straighten a little away from him. "What about Lenny?"

"Have you forgotten you were locked in that steam room with him?"

"No."

"You had to rush to his side when he was in the hospital after that collision. I'm not blind, Tee. You two are awfully close."

"We're just friends. Really." I want Joe to believe me. I want to believe myself. I struggle for the truth. "I kissed him. One time, okay?"

Joe frowns.

"I'm here with you, for heaven's sake. Sitting in *your* lap, in case you've forgotten. Can we please stop talking?"

"I haven't forgotten." He brushes his fingers through my hair and appears thoughtful. His gaze comes back to mine. "Look, Tee, my last relationship, I got burned. Bad. We were engaged until I found out she'd been lying to me about pretty much everything almost from the beginning. She'd been seeing another guy, one she'd been with before me, the whole time we were together."

Unbelievable! How could anyone in her right mind cheat on a guy like Joe?

"You've got a lot of secrets, Tee."

"I haven't lied to you." Had I?

"Crazy as this may sound, I believe you."

"But you don't trust me." How can he when I haven't given him a reason to?

"I want to."

I get off his lap and pull my chair close to his. I need to put that bit of distance between us so I can think how to say this. "Joe, the reason I can't tell you about everything, honestly, is for your own protection. For mine, too. If anything happened to you because of me, because of the things I'm looking into—"

"Okay, can you at least tell me this: Does it have something to do with those guys you were spying on that night in the parking lot? Those Albanian guys?"

If Joe had already figured out that much, my confirming it wouldn't make any difference, would it? "Yes. Partly."

"I thought so."

"It's...complicated."

"That's why you carry a gun now? Because of them?"

"Partly. Yes."

Joe stands and carries his plate and mug into the kitchen. I follow with my own. After we set our dishes in the sink, he hesitates for a moment before he turns to face me. "I don't want anything to happen to you. You do what you need to do to stay safe."

He brushes his lips against mine, retrieves his belongings from the living room and lets himself out.

I stand there wondering. Was that a goodbye kiss?

Dear Reader,

Thank you for reading. If you enjoyed this book, please post a review at the site where you purchased it or on Goodreads.com. Please share your enjoyment with other readers you think might like it. Another installment of Tee's adventures entitled KILLER BEANS is in the works.

You can check out my other books and learn more about me at the following links.

Happy reading!
AJ

Follow me on Twitter:
@ajtillock and @barbmeyers

Visit my web site:
http://www.barbarameyers.com

www.ingramcontent.com/pod-product-compliance
Lightning Source LLC
Chambersburg PA
CBHW031659170626
46808CB00005B/1524